Call Me Pomeroy

By James Hanna

Copyright ©2015 James Hanna

Published by Sand Hill Review Press
www.sandhillreviewpress.com,
P.O. Box 1275, San Mateo, CA 94401
(415) 297-3571

Library of Congress Control Number: 2015932221
Fiction/Satire

ISBN: 978-1-937818-15-9 Perfect Bound

Cover design: Backspace Ink
Cover illustration by Getty Images

Call Me Pomeroy is a work of fiction. Its characters, scenes and locales are the product of the author's imagination or are used fictitiously. Any similarity of fictional characters to people living or dead is purely coincidental.

SHRP

Sand Hill Review Press

This book is dedicated to

E. Branden Hart
Kari Totah
Robert Rossi

E. Branden Hart is the executive editor at *Empty Sink Publishing,* an online journal for intellectual deviants. He discovered Pomeroy and encouraged me to write sequels.

Kari Totah is my former office partner at the San Francisco Probation Department. Her experiences in Ireland were a valuable contribution to "Pomeroy and the New World Order."

Robert Rossi is my ex-partner at the San Francisco Probation Department. His ribald sense of humor greatly inspired the creation of Pomeroy. We met probationers like Pomeroy—delusional and gifted, kind, smart, but without a certain self-control and with a penchant to swing at windmills—perfect ingredients for a compelling story.

Sand Hill Review Press would like to thank and acknowledge *Empty Sink Publishing*. Three out of the four chapters in the Pomeroy saga by James Hanna were first published in that literary journal.

"Call Me Pomeroy"
First published in *Empty Sink Publishing* 2013

"Pomeroy and the Rights of Man"
First published in *Empty Sink Publishing* 2014

"Pomeroy and the New World Order" First published in *Empty Sink Publishing* 2014

"Pomeroy and the Last Supper"
No prior publication.

http://emptysinkpublishing.com (The magazine for intellectual deviants.)

And what rough beast, its hour come round at last,
Slouches towards Bethlehem to be born?

William Butler Yeats

Introduction

I first met Ol' Pomeroy on October 2, 2013. It's easy for me to pin down the date because I wrote quite a few emails about him that evening.

See, I had just embarked on a new venture with my long-time friend, Adam Dubbin. We were putting together a literary and arts magazine called Empty Sink Publishing, and by the beginning of October of that year, we already had plenty of material for the first issue. Jim had just sent us "Call Me Pomeroy," which is the first story in this book. It was over eleven thousand words—much longer than anything else we planned to publish, so we discussed writing Jim and telling him we'd consider it for our next issue, but that it would be too much work for the first one.

Instead, I started reading the story. The way I figured it, if it was crap, I'd be able to tell within a couple of pages, we could reject it, and that would be that--end of story.

So I read. I got through half of "Call Me Pomeroy" before dinner, rushed through a meal with my wife, and finished the rest immediately after. I'll let the email I sent to Adam speak for how much I loved this story:

FROM: E. Branden Hart
TO: Adam Dubbin
SUBJECT: RE: Empty Sink Fiction Submission_Call Me Pomeroy
DATE: Wed, Oct 2, 2013 at 9:29 PM

I want to publish Pomeroy. I want to publish it in the first issue, in its entirety. This piece should not be serialized--I don't care how long it is.

I want to feature it prominently, and make it "Editor's Choice," if not just for fiction, for the whole damn issue.

Do NOT start reading this piece unless you have an hour to finish it. It needs to be read in its entirety. You need to read it when you're ready to have a good time--I'M SERIOUS. Don't read this until you're relaxed and ready to have some fun. After the day's work is over, with a beer. Or four.

It isn't a story that should be read in parts. And it is the best thing that's been submitted to us so far. I have no idea why this person is coming to us for publication, but if we pass this up, we might as well shut down the site.

Can you tell I liked it?

My first impression was two-fold: "Call Me Pomeroy" was the most well-written submission we'd had thus far, and it was absolutely hilarious. I'd never encountered a character with such blind optimism and phallic orientation as Pomeroy.

But as I read the story again, I realized that something deeper draws me to Pomeroy: he speaks the truth. His thoughts about women may be antiquated, and he might be a tad narcissistic, and his optimism might be so blind that it leads him to the edge of the cliff, but he's *honest*. And in telling his story, James Hanna sheds a little light on some truths in the world that are difficult to confront.

Now don't get me wrong: Pomeroy is a fun guy to be around, and you're going to enjoy your time with him. He'll make you laugh like a hyena, even at things that you later may be ashamed you laughed at. Pomeroy is truly a character, and in creating him, James Hanna has introduced an anti-hero for the twenty-first century.

I'm truly grateful to have played a small part in Pomeroy's journey. He's an icon we didn't know we needed, and he's arrived right on time.

—E. Branden Hart
Executive Editor, EmptySinkPublishing.com
11/2/2014

Table of Contents

1.
Call Me Pomeroy

I TELL FOLKS TO CALL ME POMEROY. That's a whole lot better than Eddie Beasley—the name I was born with fifty-five years ago.

Pomeroy has class, style, and strut. And I ain't got no choice 'cept to strut. Don't matter that I'm homeless. Don't matter that I wear polyester bell-bottoms. Don't matter that I act a little crazy now and again. Because I'm a *stud*—I'm a *star*. And sooner or later, a star's gotta shine.

Now a star's gotta share himself—that's how it is. So last week I put an ad in a swingers' mag. An ad for *straight* sex—none of this bi shit for me. Hell, I don't even buy muscle balm unless it's *Ben Straight*. So the ad *told* it straight.

Picture me one and all, it read. *I'm six foot six with broad shoulders, a narrow waist, and thighs like a stallion. I'm available for one-on-ones or threesomes. I can handle two women at once. And I look just like Queequeg out of Moby Dick. Contact General Post Office, 101 Hyde Street, San Francisco.* Got a hundred responses, but I only answered a couple of 'em. Sometimes, describin' yourself is enough.

11

They got me on parole, you know. For *statutory rape* if you can believe that. They could have gotten me for battery. They could have gotten me for assault. They could have gotten me for threatenin' a cop. Crimes like that are worth braggin' about. But they got me for *statutory rape*. No matter that the little spinner lied about her age. No matter that I wasn't her first by a long shot. No matter that she rode me like a jockey while all the time squealin' like a pig. Hell, she practically raped *me*. And then, when she turned eighteen, she came to see me at San Quentin— guess I must have spoiled her for other men. But I wouldn't have nothin' more to do with her. When a woman puts Pomeroy in jail, Pomeroy cuts her off. I told her she'd have to make do with my mug shot and a dildo.

They gave me a psych eval while I was at Quentin. The psychiatrist looked at me like I was a bug on the wall and said, "Ahem, Mr. Beasley, you got yerself a narcissistic personality disorder."

"What?!" I said.

"Ahem, Mr. Beasley, you got yourself an explosive disorder. And an antisocial personality to boot."

That's psychs for you—they gotta make a problem out of everythin'. Just 'cause a man likes to fuck and fight don't mean he's got problems. And just 'cause he can think for *himself* don't mean he's antisocial.

I SLEEP IN THE MULTIPURPOSE CENTER on Fifth and Bryant across from the San Francisco Hall of Justice. My parole officer reserved me a bed there—no waitin' in shelter lines for ol' Pomeroy. The shitkickers there all know me well. Whenever I walk into the building they say, "Pomeroy, you're the *man*. You're the *stud*. How's it hangin', *Pomeroy*?"

I play the game. "Loose and full of juice," I say and they all laugh. But they're full of shit. And they know that I *know* that they're full of shit. They just don't want to mess with the baddest dude in San Francisco.

I got out of Quentin a month ago so I'm still kinda trippin' on freedom. The nicest thing about it is that I can eat what I want to eat. So I start each day with a hearty breakfast at the Sunshine Café on Polk Street. No soup lines at Saint Anthony's for Pomeroy. I have the same breakfast every mornin'—two eggs over easy, hash browns, sausages, and wheat toast. And three cups of steamin' hot coffee. That's as close to heaven as a man's gonna get. And there's no point in messin' with heaven.

The waitresses there have all got to know me, and whenever I walk in they say, "*Pomeroy*. You want the usual, Pomeroy?"

"Does a bear leave turds in the woods?" I answer. They laugh like crazy at that old chestnut—that's 'cause they're really nice. They don't even mind that I sit there for hours and read every page of the San Francisco Chronicle. First I read the sports pages and then I read about the occupation movements over in Oakland and The Embarcadero. And once I'm done, I leave 'em a ten-dollar tip.

When I've had my breakfast, I go over to Market Street and do a little panhandlin'. I always pick the tourists 'cause they don't know what to expect. I say to 'em, "*Oy*. Can you spare me some cash for a beef burrito?" I hate any kind of burrito, but I've got to tell 'em somethin'. And when they try to buy me off with a buck or two—that's when I go crazy. *"Five,"* I tell 'em. *"I gotta have five."* And then I start spittin' like a faucet, rollin' my eyes, and lurchin' about like a zombie. So I always *get* my five dollars. But I don't hustle more cash than I need—unlike *some* folks. And once I've picked up fifteen or twenty dollars, I get the hell out of there. No point waitin' for the cops to show. The cops know me too well as it is.

When I'm done panhandlin', I walk over to the public library. I don't go there to sleep or shoot up in the bathroom—I go there to *read*. 'Cause Pomeroy ain't no illiterate, crack-smokin' bum. He's a coffee-sippin', Shakespeare-quotin' bum. That's why I was assigned to the library at Quentin. That's why *nobody* fools me—a man who likes to read has got his *own* mind.

Now usually, I read the classics 'cause none of the modern writers are worth a shit. Except maybe Charles Frazier. *Cold Mountain* got it right. Don't be dyin' for no slave ownin' one-percenters. But I prefer the classics, and I read 'em 'til the pages fall out. *Paradise Lost* I've read a dozen times 'cause the *devil* got it right, too. Don't be kissin' ass in heaven when you can rule the whole underworld. Makes sense to ol' Pomeroy.

I kinda like Joyce's *Ulysses*—not the story but the way he tells it. There ain't much story to it. An ol' boy wakes up, wanders around Dublin, sees a pretty crippled girl, and jacks off. And then he goes to a pub and pisses off a racist. And then he goes home and has a cup of tea. Meanwhile, his wife is lyin' in bed ticklin' her minnow. Guess the ol' boy couldn't deal with her. Guess *pocket pool* was all he could handle. She shoulda had a dose of Pomeroy. I'd have had her shriekin' like a banshee.

I like the poets too—especially that Yeats dude, his poem about mere anarchy and all. *And what rough beast, his hour come at last, slouches towards Bethlehem to be born.* I ain't sure what all that means, but I like it anyhow. That's one big-dicked poem.

I'm a hell of a poet myself. I recite my stuff at The City Lights Bookstore when they have their open mic readings, and I strum my guitar while I read that shit. While I was there last week, I read 'em a poem I wrote about that Bush dude—the fucker who stole himself a whole *presidency*. I wrote it five years ago, but that didn't make no difference. The crowd was stompin' and hollerin' before I even finished the first verse.

> *This man we call a president*
> *   is just a piece of shit.*
> *He ain't got no intelligence.*
> *He got no soul or wit.*
> *He'll call on you to sacrifice.*
> *He'll send your sons to die.*
> *But his hands are full of money*
> *   and his heart is full of lies.*

Well, the shitkickers there went ballistic on me. *"Tell it like it is, Pomeroy! Tell it like it is!"* they all hollered. So I read 'em a bit more.

Now he'll claim to be a Christian.
Now he'll say his soul is filled.
But all he really worships is the
corporate dollar bill.

I had to *stop* there even though I had forty-seven more verses. Because the women were about to rip off their bras and shake their titties at me. Write yourself a poem—even a fucked-up poem—and women are gonna mob you. I was damn lucky to get out with my bellbottoms still on.

TWICE A MONTH, I go to the General Assistance Office where I pick up a check for two- hundred thirty bucks. I cash it at the Sunshine Café, and then I look carefully at the money. Ain't it amazin'—the shitbags who got their faces on money? There's Jackson, an Indian murderer. There's Jefferson, a slave owner. There's Grant, a drunk and a butcher for the cotton guilds. And that goddamn Lincoln was the worst of them all. Killed himself half a million people just so he could keep the cotton tariffs jacked up. Talk about a one-percenter.

But that's the way things go in this country. Steal a little and they'll throw you in jail. Steal a lot and you'll get your face put on money. Guess it don't hurt a fucker to be on the right side of history.

Hell, even that Kennedy dude got himself a fifty-cent piece. I remember his speech when he became president. "Ask *not* what your country can do for you," he said. "Ask what *you* can do for your country." What a steamin' pile of crap *that* was. You might as well ask the one-percenters to pick your pocket and kill you in their wars. *Fuck* that shit. But they're all pretty much the same—Kennedy, Jesse Jackson, even Bill Clinton. They want you to be faithful to some cause or other when they can't even be faithful to their *own wives*. If a man wants *my* vote, he can damn well keep his pecker in his *pants*.

WHEN I'M DONE at the library, it's almost dark. That's when I go to the Multipurpose Center and chill out with the shitkickers. Usually, we watch television—*Survivor* if it's on. I like bettin' on who gets voted off. Usually, I win but when I don't win the shitkickers all shake their heads.

"You don't gotta pay us, Pomeroy," they say— that's 'cause they're all scared shitless of me. But I always pay up when I lose—even if it's twenty bucks. If a man don't have his dignity, he's got nothin'—hell, he may as well *be* on *Survivor*. *None* of those folks on *Survivor* have dignity—if they did they'd get voted off the first week. And it's the biggest slime balls of them all who end up with a million dollars—like maybe they took lessons from the one-percenters. They oughta call the show *Conniver*.

I like *American Idol* too. Round up a bunch of pretty looking kids, have 'em sing other people's music, and you got yourself a *show*. It's *that* easy to become a celebrity. It's *that* easy to have millions of people hollerin' out your name. Now if those pissants can make it—kids who don't even sing their own words—it's gonna be even easier for Pomeroy. The shitkickers all agree with me.

17

"You're gonna make it, Pomeroy," they say. "You're gonna make it *big*." And then I recite 'em one of my poems.

TONIGHT, THEY'RE PITCHIN' tents in Frank Ogawa Plaza over in Oakland. So tonight I ain't watchin' no pissants sing other people's music. There's better entertainment on the news—all those little spinner types wigglin' their asses to drumbeats. Makes ol' Pomeroy pitch a tent of his own. And those folks dressed like corporate zombies are a hoot. The zombies keep shoutin', *"Money makes the rules!"*— like maybe they just figured that *out*. The zombies keep shoutin', *"We're changin' the rules!"* Fuck that shit. Haven't they read *Animal Farm*? I guess not— that's a bit much to expect from a zombie. What rules are they gonna change anyhow? Ol' Pomeroy makes his own rules. 'Cause I think with my *head* and I *fuck* with my cock. There ain't a whole lot of folks who can get things in that order.

That means I gotta leave Frisco for a while. Gotta change my routine every now and then just to keep the cops guessin'. It's too easy for 'em to pin stuff on ol' Pomeroy. But the cops ain't gonna bug me in Oakland—there's too many *anarchists* there that need bustin'. And Pomeroy ain't no anarchist.

But that don't mean I'll be missin' the party—not when they got food tents set up over there. None of that vegetarian shit for me, though. They better be servin' sausages if they want to keep Pomeroy around. Gotta keep my strength up if there's fightin' to be done. Gotta keep my strength up if I'm gonna play my music. And if I get my face on the evenin' news, I might just get a recordin' contract.

So I grab my guitar and sleepin' bag and go to the San Francisco Ferry Building. And I buy me a one-way boat trip to Jack London Square. I like Jack London 'cause he told it like it is. Or like it oughta be anyhow. The ol' survival of the fittest. The law of tooth and club. That's why I read *The Sea Wolf* twenty times. That's why I'm the baddest dude on the street. That's why I'm thankful every day to be the big ol' bruiser I am. I *believe* in that survival of the fittest shit.

But things ain't that way really—that's just how they *oughta* be. Just look at that Bush dude—that fucker ain't fast, smart, *or* strong. In college, he was a fuckin' *cheerleader*. And *he* got to be president of the whole damn country. And *he* got to send folks to wars of *his* choosin'. Guess it don't hurt a man to be in good with the one-percenters. Take care of them and they'll take care of you.

Today, the bay is calm. Today, the sun is shinin' like a motherfucker. So I stand on the top deck and breathe deep of the salt air. The *top deck*—that's the only place I can get a bit of privacy. The only place I can scribble me a poem. 'Cause the women aboard the ferry are all givin' me the eye. Like maybe I'm gonna harpoon 'em with my whanger—give 'em a break from their husbands. But that's how it is when you're gonna be a star. The woman all want you to satisfy 'em.

When the boat docks in Oakland, I get off quick. Before the women have a chance to tear my pants off. And then I wander around Jack London Square. I

19

look at the shops, the bookstores, and that log cabin they shipped in from the Yukon. I look at the statue of ol' Jack. The statue looks like it's callin' me—like it's givin' me a signal. Like maybe ol' Pomeroy's time has come. I read the inscription at the base—even though I know it by heart.

I would rather be a superb meteor, every atom of me in magnificent glow, than a sleepy and permanent planet . . .

Fuck that crap. Ol' Pomeroy ain't gonna *be* no flash in the pan. Ol' Pomeroy's gonna be around for a long time.

I treat myself to lunch at the Sea Wolf Café. I order me a dozen oysters. I'm gonna need 'em when I corral those little spinners. When I'm done eatin', I walk the ten blocks to Frank Ogawa Plaza.

I hear the tent city before I see it. There's music, drums—the amplified voice of a speaker. The noise is so loud and warlike that I'm kinda disappointed when I finally see the place. There's maybe a hundred-and-fifty igloo-shaped tents all crowded together on a small patch of grass. The place looks too small to be makin' that much racket.

I walk along 14th Street then cut across the Plaza to City Hall. Michael Moore—that fucker who makes in-your-face movies—is standin' on the City Hall steps.

He's tellin' the crowd, "Today, you killed despair." He's tellin' the crowd, "Today, you killed apathy." But he also keeps talkin' about how he's eatin' too much red meat. Guess that dude could skip a few Twinkies too—he's gotta weigh 400 pounds. But it really don't matter *what* he's sayin'—the crowd, maybe a thousand people, is gonna keep on applaudin' him. He could just as well be sayin', "Today, I'm buggerin' your mothers and daughters"—they'd still be cheerin' him on. But that fucker don't fool ol' Pomeroy. I saw *real* revolutionaries in Nam—skinny little dudes who could march fifty miles on a cup of rice. I'd like to see ol' Michael Moore do that.

When ol' Michael's done speaking, some dry puss grabs the microphone—this shriveled old woman who's gotta be a hundred-and-twenty years old. She starts givin' a report about the camp: the food they got available, the medical tent, and the fliers that need distributin'. I get bored with her quick—the crowd does too—and I start wanderin' down 14th street.

The first thing I see is a column of shitkickers— Iraqi veterans against that war Bush started—and they're marchin' along all ramrod straight. They're singin' the ol' *Sound Off Cadence*—'cept they changed the words around some. I listen to 'em singin' out and then I start singin' along.

"*Corporation profits riiise. CORPORATION PROFITS RIIISE. Common people bleed and diiie. COMMON PEOPLE BLEED AND DIIIE. Sound off. ONE, TWO. Sound off! THREE, FOUR. Break it on down. ONE, TWO, THREE, FOUR. ONE TWO— THREE, FOUR!*"

They say Nam, another fucked up war, fucked me up too. But that ain't the case—even though I did a couple of tours there after flunkin' outta high school in Michigan City, Indiana. The truth is ol' Pomeroy fucked up Nam. Scored me a whole lot of Asian pussy and mailed home a fortune in artifacts that I took from the Buddhist temples. I mailed home a ton of gold too—pried it from the teeth of those little fuckers we shot dead.

So it don't hurt a man to be fightin' in a king's war—not if he stays on the ball. Not if he's gettin' some gravy for *himself*. But I sing along with the war veterans anyhow—clappin' my hands and rollin' my eyes. I keep repeatin' the *Sound Off Cadence*. 'Cause I don't want 'em thinkin' I'm no undercover cop.

When the press folks start crowdin' the veterans—they're lookin' for any old story to pounce on—I start gettin' bored. The veterans keep talkin' about how this is the only occupation they feel comfortable with, and the reporters keep askin' 'em a lot of half-assed questions. So I wander on over to the tent city, buy me an ounce of weed, and look over the little spinners who are givin' me the eye.

After awhile, I get kinda hungry—those oysters are wearin' off quick—so I walk on over to the food tent. They ain't servin' sausages there so I have me a bowl of soup.

I HANG AROUND the tent city for four or five days—smokin' weed, strummin' my guitar, and checkin' out the spinners. They look kinda grubby from all the marchin' they been doing. Some of 'em even smell, which is kind of a turn-off. And the placards they're carryin' don't help much either.

No Justice, No Peace, the placards read—now what kind of bullshit is that? Ol' Pomeroy can *always* do justice to a piece of *ass*. But if I screwed too many of 'em, there *still* wouldn't be no peace. Not when they started fightin' over me. So I keep to myself, strum my guitar, and score all the weed I can get.

On my fifth afternoon in the tent city, a reporter comes around, sees me writin' a poem, and pokes a microphone in my face.

"What's *your* message here, sir?" he asks.

I start to act all mysterious, like maybe I'm some kind of holy man, and I strike a couple of chords on my guitar.

"To become a vessel to life," I reply. I heard David Carradine say that once on *Kung Fu*—that martial arts series from the seventies. I still watch the re-runs every chance I get. 'Cause I *like* a dude who can spout wisdom *and* kick ass.

Don't know what kinda vessel *Carradine* was, though. Not when he was into bondage. Not when he hung himself in a hotel room just to get a hard-on. Ain't no hard-on in the world worth riskin' your life for—not even a *Pomeroy* hard-on. Unless maybe if you're a woman on the receiving end of it.

After a minute or two, the reporter takes my picture. I ask him for a copy and he promises to send one to my post office address. That oughta look good on my album cover—ol' Pomeroy standin' up for the workingman. May as well act like Woody Guthrie while I'm out here.

When the reporter finishes copying my address, he goes hurryin' off. That's 'cause Frank Ogawa Plaza is packed with people now. *There's gonna be a strike on Oakland*, the loudspeaker announces. Don't know how these fuckers can strike if they don't have jobs, but it looks like they're gonna have one anyhow. So I shoulder my guitar, put away my poem, and walk on over to join them.

I MARCH ALONG 14th Street with the crowd—all the time puffin' out my chest, strummin' my guitar, and singin', "This land is *our* land." And all these folks keep crowdin' behind me, clappin' their hands and singin' along. Oughta have a bodyguard to keep 'em all away from me. Or maybe I'll just round 'em up and turn 'em into a cult.

There's a lot to be said for havin' yourself a cult. Folks will give you all their savings to work for you for nothin'. And all the while, you'll be fuckin' the wives. There ain't no sweeter deal than *that*.

But there ain't no challenge to brainwashin' folks. Hell, there's fuckers all over the street shoutin', "*Socialism now!*"—like they got too much Obama on the brain. I holler along with 'em 'cause I don't want 'em thinkin' I'm workin' for the pigs, but ol' Pomeroy ain't no *socialist*. A General Assistance check twice a month—that's all ol' Pomeroy needs. Gotta keep myself lean and hungry if I'm gonna to hustle my music. And when I've made me a million or two, I ain't giving *squat* to no crack-smokin' lay abouts. Gonna buy me a Lamborghini, dress up in a sharkskin suit, and score me some thousand-dollar-a-night hookers. Women with *class*. Women who won't bother me when I'm done screwin' 'em. So *fuck* that socialism shit.

I march with the demonstrators 'til late afternoon, strummin' my guitar, fightin' off women, and lettin' the news crews put me on television. But around 3:00

p.m., a bunch of *anarchists* come and mess things up. There's fifty or sixty of the fuckers—all dressed in black and wearin' ski masks—and they think they can kick ass. So they start throwin' chairs at this Whole Foods store and they start stompin' on the picket fence surroundin' it and one of 'em takes a can of spray paint and writes *STRIKE* on the store window. And then the news folk, who are always lookin' for another story, *forget* ol' Pomeroy and point their cameras at the *anarchists*.

By now, ol' Pomeroy's gettin' pissed off. The rest of the marchers are gettin' pissed off too.

"Show us your faces!" they shout. *"You're better than this!"* they shout.

Then this solid-looking dude beside me hollers, *"These assholes are stealing the show!"*

The dude grabs a steel pole layin' on the ground, twirls it around Ninja-style, and chases all sixty of the anarchists away. Some revolutionaries *they* are—but the damage is done. The news teams are all chasin' after the fuckers, beggin' them for a statement. And the goddamn store has closed itself down. Just when ol' Pomeroy was gonna get himself a key lime tart.

Things ain't no better when we get to the Wells Fargo bank a few blocks down the street. The anarchists are rallyin' there—breakin' the ATM machines and writin' *FUCK THIS BANK* on the windows they ain't smashed yet. On top of that, they're grabbin' cameras from the news folk and rippin' out the film—film that's got *Pomeroy* on it. The fuckers keep shoutin' how banks got bailed out while they got sold out, but that don't make a *bit* of sense. Not when they're wearin' them expensive Air Jordan Nikes, it don't.

Well, ol' Pomeroy's ready to kick himself some ass, but the rest of the marchers are puttin' a lid on things. That's 'cause the cops are all standin' behind the bank window—like maybe they're scared of them pissant anarchists. So the rest of the marchers start grabbin' the fuckers, yellin' in their faces, and tellin' 'em they're gonna make citizen arrests. But the anarchists are long gone before any of 'em can get copped. The fuckers can *fly* on those Air Jordans.

WHEN IT GETS TO BE 11:00 P.M., ol' Pomeroy's ready to crash. Most of the marchers have gone on home, and I ain't been signed to no recordin' contract yet. So I walk on over to the Traveler's Aid Building on 16th Street. Ol' Pomeroy's slept there many a time, but the protesters have taken the place over now— *liberated* it in the name of the people. They've even hung this big banner outside that says *OCCUPY EVERYTHING.*

All ol' Pomeroy wants to occupy is a *bed*, but it don't look like I'll be gettin' no more sleep in *that* building. There's maybe three hundred protesters in front of the place—most of 'em anarchists wearin' black—and they've set a fuckin' barricade on fire. And the cops, who have finally grown themselves a set of balls, are startin' to close in.

The cops have formed into a double-line and they're all wearin' riot helmets, spit-shields, and bulletproof vests. And they're poppin' air grenades at the protesters and shootin' 'em with rubber bullets and the protesters keep hollerin', *"Banks got bailed out—we got sold out!"* The protesters haven't even changed their *material,* but there's news crews everywhere puttin' the fuckers on film. *What kind of shit is that?!*

After a few minutes, the place is in fuckin' bedlam. There's protesters throwin' bottles at cops. There's protesters chokin' on tear gas and smoke. There's cops hookin' fuckers up and haulin' 'em off to the meat wagons. And over near the Traveler's Aid Building, some anarchists are stagin' a show of their *own.* There's maybe twenty or thirty of the fuckers all standin' in a circle, and they've cornered themselves a cop. The cop's got wide hips so she's gotta be a woman, but the anarchists are shovin' her back and forth anyhow. They look like a wolf pack that's captured a deer.

Ol' Pomeroy decides that's *enough* of that shit. Can't let no woman get beat up even if she *is* a cop. That's a damn waste of good pussy. So I stash my guitar under a bush, elbow my way into the circle, and hoist the bitch up on my shoulders—like maybe I'm a fireman. Well, the anarchists start lookin' at me kinda dumbstruck so I give 'em the ol' thumbs-up. Like I'm gonna haul this bitch off to a park and have my way with her. Pay her back *good* for protectin' the banks.

Soon, the anarchists start hootin' at me and givin' me the ol' thumbs-up. One of them even steps forward, this tall-ass dude wearing one of them Anonymous Guy Fawkes masks. The mask looks kinda like the devil, but it ain't no improvement when the fucker takes it off and lets me see his face. His jaw is so weak that he looks like a mole and his eyes are bulgin' out like Ping-Pong balls.

Well, the fucker licks his lips, like he likes the taste of tear gas, and he starts talkin' to me in this highbrow *English* accent. "Who might you be, noble warrior?" he says. "And why have you hoisted that dyke on your shoulders?" Dude acts like a silver-spooner who'd like to hide his roots.

"Pomeroy," I tell him. "Pomeroy's the name. And I'm gonna show this bitch some liquid assets."

Well, the anarchists start laughin' like crazy and pattin' me on the chest, so I grin like a possum and I carry the bitch across the street. Don't know if she's dyke or not, but that don't make no never mind at all. She wouldn't be the *first* dyke ol' Pomeroy's turned straight.

I drop the bitch onto the sidewalk and I look her over good. She's a bit too heavy for Pomeroy's taste so I tell her to haul ass. But when she removes her spit-shield and looks at me, it don't look like she wants to go *nowhere*. Not when her nostrils are flarin' like a racehorse, it don't. It looks like she wants to fall to her knees, tear off my pants, and give me a knob job right there on the street. But before she can grab my belt, I hear the cops yellin' at each other.

"Get him, get him, get him!"

"Who?!"

"That big dude! Looks like a South Sea islander! The bastard's kidnapped Nora!"

I look away from the bitch, hopin' she don't rip off my zipper, and I see a dozen cops bearin' down on me. One of 'em swings a baton at my head, but I push him onto his ass. Ol' Pomeroy's faster than a rattler's tongue. But the cops are all over me now—the chickenshits ain't linin' up to fight like they do on *Kung Fu*. A blow stings my neck and, next thing I know, my hands are pushin' away the *sidewalk*.

I hear Nora, or whatever the fuck her name is, screamin', "*Don't hurt him*," like maybe she's still hopin' for a pokin'. Like maybe she's wantin' a piece of a *star*. 'Cause lights all around me are hoppin' like shit and they kinda remind me of flashbulbs.

JAIL AIN'T SHIT—take it from a dude who knows his jails. But if you gotta be in jail, you can do a lot worse than the Santa Rita Lockup. The place has state-of-the-art housing units, solar paneling, and it looks like a fuckin' community college. And the bed pods got exercise bikes where ol' Pomeroy can crack off laps—keep in shape for all them women. But it'd be a whole lot better if I didn't have to share it with a bunch of anarchists. Those fuckers have gathered in the TV area and they're singin' *God Bless America* at the top of their lungs. Just when ol' Pomeroy wanted to go switch on *Bonanza*. Fuck that shit.

But maybe I won't be around here long—listenin' to these assholes who can't even hold a tune. 'Cause before I even have my breakfast, the desk officer tells me to report to the attorneys' module. And when I get there, my parole officer is waitin' to see me. Her name is Jessica Jimenez, and she's a hot-blooded Latina with smolderin' eyes and a damn fine ass for a woman of fifty. She's gotta be a dyke or I'd have screwed her by now, but that don't make a bit of never mind. Jessica's always been good to Pomeroy and Pomeroy takes care of his own.

When I enter the module, ol' Jessica's sittin' there writin' into her logbook. She's swingin' her leg as she writes—*praise the Lord*. 'Cause she's wearin' these alligator pumps that give ol' Pomeroy a fat one. But when she looks at me, I kinda lose my woody. Ol' Jessica's got this way of lookin' at you that can make you feel conspicuous. Like maybe you're a stray dog that pissed all over her carpet.

Ol' Jessica gives me the once over then she draws herself a deep breath. She always draws a deep breath before speakin' to me—that's 'cause she's a Latina. She's a bit of a drama queen, ol' Jessica.

"Head-ward," she says finally—that's how she pronounces my name. "*Head-ward Beasley. What* have you been up to, señor?"

I sit across from her and scoot up close to the table. That's 'cause her husky accent is makin' me stiff again.

"I'm a *rising star*, Miss Jimenez," I say.

Jessica frowns and closes her logbook. Her alligator pump is danglin' from her toe.

"Head-ward," she says to me sternly. "We have talked about this *before*. I am *not* here to star in your schoolboy daydreams."

Well, that kinda ticks ol Pomeroy off. If Jessica ain't gonna give me a whirl, she oughtn't be statin' opinions like that. Ol' Jessica's a bit like a mare that needs breakin'—she just ain't found the right man to slip it to her yet.

But ol' Pomeroy needs to slip out of this *jail*—get himself back on television. So I don't press the point.

I just give ol' Jessica a wink. Ain't a woman alive who can resist a wink from ol' Pomeroy.

"I apologize, Miss Jimenez," I say and I *mean* it. "You give me a bit of a charge, is all."

Ol' Jessica shrugs, like she ain't quite heard me, and opens her briefcase. "The *charges*, Head-ward, are trespass, false imprisonment, resisting peace officers."

She hands me the police report, but I don't bother lookin' at it. Got my eyes on her alligator pump.

"Mi amor," she says. "What were you doing with that policewoman on your back? Didn't you think that would get you noticed?"

"No," I reply. "I was *hopin'* it would."

Ol' Jessica kinda shakes her head. "I know you are a *fine* musician, Head-ward. But that's *not* a good way to get noticed."

Now that's a shitload if ever I heard one, but I don't wanna be disrespectful to ol' Jessica. So I address her like a gentleman. "There *ain't* no bad way to get noticed, Miss Jimenez," I say. "Ain't you read Oscar Wilde?"

Ol' Jessica groans and nibbles her pen. The bitch has teeth like pearls. "Do you think I'm *illiterate*, Head-ward?" she says, her voice all touchy now. "You *always* want me to read something."

"Gotta work on your *mind*, Miss Jimenez," I say. "Your ass don't need no seasonin'."

Ol' Jessica covers her mouth with her hand, but I hear her gigglin' anyway. The woman has the hots for me and don't even know it. But she does know ol'

Pomeroy don't follow rules. Not when it's *motherfuckers* who make 'em up.

When I hand ol' Jessica back her report, her hand kinda lingers on mine. "*Your* season will come," she says to me gently. "I'm sure it will, Head-ward. I am sure you will have all the groupies you want. Now will you *please* stop staring at my foot?" She looks at me like I accidently brushed her tit then studies the police report again. "I've *never* had a client quite like you, Head-ward."

"That's 'cause I'm up and comin'," I say.

Ol' Jessica frowns so I *know* she's gettin' tired of them jokes. But she pats me on the wrist, and her palm is cooler 'n a cucumber. "You'll be getting out this evening, Head-ward. The district attorney is dropping *all* charges on you. I told him you're a *very special* case."

I thank ol' Jessica and shake her hand, and she tells me to *please* be more careful. I promise I will, but she's gotta know I'm shittin' her. 'Cause a man who don't take chances is gonna end up broke.

As I walk back down the range, a couple of trustees start grinnin' at me—a pair of shitkickers who oughta keep moppin' the floor. "*Whooee*," says one of 'em.

I stop walkin' and I look at him—the same way I'd look at a turd. "Can I help you?" I ask.

Well, the dumb-ass fucker starts strokin' his mop handle—like maybe he's well-endowed. "Damn fine ass on your parole officer," he says. "She wears that skirt like it's a coat of paint. You are *one lucky dude*, bro."

Well, I just stand there, my hands on my hips, and I look the asshole straight in the eye. "You wanna be wearin' that *bucket*?" I ask him. "Your head oughta fit in it nice."

The fucker pauses, like he's seriously considerin' the question, then he answers in a shaky-ass voice. "Well, no. . . No, I don't want to be wearin' no bucket." He's tryin' to act real slick and all but he's ready to piss his pants.

"You don't wanna wear that bucket," I say, "you'll stop talkin' that way about Miss Jimenez."

I leave the fucker to crap his pants and I walk on back to my bed pod. Ol' Jessica may be full of shit, but ain't *nobody* gonna diss that bitch. I'd fight an army for her any day.

THEY LET ME OUT OF JAIL around 6:00 p.m., and I catch the BART back to Oakland. I find my guitar where I left it, under a bush near the Traveler's Aid Building, and I sling it over my shoulder and head on back to Frank Ogawa Plaza.

The place is still packed with tents and protesters—I guess 'cause the police are too chickenshit to clear it out. And although it's nearly midnight, there's singin' and guitar strummin' going on everywhere. But the music ain't worth a *shit*. Ain't none of these fuckers heard of Jefferson Airplane, The Band, Bob Dylan? They could use a dose of ol' Dylan here, but I wouldn't hold my breath waiting for *Dylan* to show up. The last I saw of *that* fucker, he was sellin' women's underwear on television.

Well, before I can even settle down—before I can even find me a place to crash—a bunch of anarchists come runnin' up to me. That tall dude, the one with the bulgin' eyeballs, is among 'em and the fucker is shoutin' in his highfalutin English voice.

"Salute noble Samson!" he shouts. "The bloke knocked out ten cops with the jawbone of an ass—all for the people! Knocked them cold, he did! And he's been sitting in jail—a living hell—all for the sake of the people! Salute noble Samson, my friends!"

Well, the fucker starts salutin' me like maybe I'm Che Guevara, and the rest of the assholes start givin' me the ol' thumbs-up again. But I just stand there and hold onto my guitar. I don't mind gettin' saluted and all, but not by some pissant who can't even handle jail. Jail ain't shit, but it ain't hell either. Hell is a cute little blonde without a hole.

Well, the fucker introduces himself as Charlemagne of all people and he invites me to dinner. And before I can tell him to fuck off, he takes me by the elbow and guides me to his tent: a big-ass teepee that's five times the size of any of the other tents. There's this whoppin' gas grill in front of it—it looks kinda like a robot—and ol' Pomeroy can smell steaks cookin'.

Now I ain't about to eat with that fucker—not if he's gonna call himself Charlemagne—but then I spot somethin' that changes my mind. Attendin' to the grill is the cutest little spinner ol' Pomeroy's ever seen. With her deep brown eyes and mahogany skin, with her braids falling down to her heart-shaped butt, she looks exactly like Pocahontas. And the bitch looks durable, sinewy-strong, like she's ready to handle some *Pomeroy* sex. *A damn fine piece of ass.* So I decide to stick around for dinner, after all. Give the bitch a break.

After Pocahontas serves us the meal—all the time givin' me the eye—I stare at my food so as not to appear too horny. Got me a prime cut of beef to work on, a Mason jar of Falcon Ridge Chardonnay, and some puffy-ass shit that's got to be Yorkshire pudding. That Charlemagne fucker eats well for a revolutionary—too damn well—'cause I hear him burpin' like a blowfish while he's swallowin' down the chardonnay.

After finishing the wine, the dude smacks his lips loud and starts talkin' about himself. Turns out he's from Manchester, which is somewhere near Wales. Turns out his father owns a piece of The Beatles. Turns out he graduated from Oxford with a degree in the classics. And then, having jack shit to do, he came over here to start shakin' things up. "Whacking the piggies" is how he puts it, like he's been listenin' to too much George Harrison.

Well, there just ain't no shuttin' that fucker up— talk about the jawbone of an ass. He keeps talkin' about Saint Crispin's Day—that battle speech from *Henry The Fifth*. He keeps talkin' about slayin' the Philistines. He keeps talkin' about the siege of Troy. So Pomeroy just grins, takes off his shirt, and flexes his muscles like mighty Odysseus. 'Cause ol' Pocahontas is wet for me now and I'm gonna score that bitch before the week is out. Give her a whirl around the ol' totem pole. Fuck 'em while they're hot—that's Pomeroy's motto.

So I don't say nothing—I let the fucker talk. He tells me the anarchists ain't worth a shit—not without no champion, they ain't. Not without a spark to light their powder. Not without some big ol' bruiser to lead 'em in the charge.

"It was blokes of your mettle," he says, "who dumped the first box of tea into Boston Harbor, who fired the first shots at Lexington and Concord, who warned John Hancock that King George was coming."

Well, I keep on sittin' there, noddin' my head, and I don't say nothin'. *Screw* John Hancock—the fucker wasn't *worth* savin'. All he did was sign a piece of paper, develop gout, and jack himself off in Congress. *John Hancock*—the name kinda says it all. But I ain't averse to no midnight ride—not if it's ol' Pocahontas I'm mountin'. The bitch needs a pokin'— that's for sure. A *long* damn pokin'. And ol' Pomeroy ain't no Minuteman.

I pick up my guitar, mostly to shut the fucker up, and play him some *kick-ass* songs. I play *Masters of War*. I play *The Battle Hymn of The Republic*. I play *Blowing in the Wind*—now ain't that a lark. The only blowin' I want is from ol' Pocahontas who's ready to cream her undies. But my music is makin' that Charlemagne asshole talk all the more.

He tells me I'm a mighty musician. He tells me I play like an angel. He tells me his father will give me a recordin' contract *for sure*. Makes me feel kinda bad that I'm gonna borrow his girlfriend. But what the fuck—ol' Pomeroy don't stand on no ceremony. Not even when his future's on the line. 'Cause destiny is destiny and ass is ass.

I HANG AROUND TENT CITY for another week, strummin' my guitar, singin' *Hard Rain*, and actin' like I'm Paul Revere. But what I'm reverin' is ol' Pocahontas. Charlemagne tells me she used to be a dancer, but gave up the stage to join the revolution. "Seize a higher calling," he says. But my Johnson is what she'll be seizin' before long—there ain't no mistakin' the sweat on her lip, the heavin' of her breasts, or the way her hands tremble whenever she serves me my mornin' coffee. It wouldn't be *merciful* of me not to screw her—not when she's starvin' for the ol' bologna pony. And I ain't talkin' about *Charlemagne's* bologna—the dude oughta be on meds. 'Cause every fuckin' day he sits outside his tent talkin' crap to his fellow anarchists.

He lectures 'em about diversity of tactics. He lectures 'em about the bank bailout. He cautions them about careful recruitment, so no undercover cops will sneak into their organization. And he says the Black Bloc Anarchists—that's what these fuckers call themselves—won't abandon none of their soldiers on the field of battle. Ain't that a load of shit? These trust fund fuckers wouldn't have lasted a day in Nam. But I don't say nothin'. I just nod my head, drink the fucker's wine, and wait for my shot at Pocahontas. 'Cause it's pussy that raises ol' Pomeroy's flagpole. Pussy ain't *never* let me down. The worst I've had has been *terrific*.

Whenever Charlemagne's done jackin' his jaws for the day, he asks me to play 'em some marchin' type music. So one day I throw in a ditty I been workin' on. I call it *Ants in My Pants* 'cause ol' Pomeroy's like a rollin' stone. Once he's fucked all the babes, he heads on down the highway.

Well, I start off with some silly ass shit—just to get the fuckers laughin'—and then I throw in some *Guthrie* type lyrics. By the time I get done, every one of them anarchists are clappin' along and singin', "*Doo, doo, doo.*" And ol' Pocahontas is drippin' like a sponge and filmin' my ass with an iPhone. I don't remember all the verses—there's ninety-seven of 'em in all—but the ones I sang go somethin' like this:

Well, the law says I'm a pervert
"Doo, doo, doo"
And the girls say I'm a cheat
"Doo, doo, doo"
'Cause I live on orange sherbet
And I like to beat my meat.

But I go to church on Sunday
"Doo, doo , doo"
And I find myself a nook
"Doo, doo, doo"
Where I eat my chili peppers
And I catch up on my books.

And I won't dance.
"No, he won't dance."
Got ants in my pants.
No, I won't dance.
Got ants inside my pants.

Now there's a rumble in the city

"Doo, doo, doo"
And a rumble in the dale
"Doo, doo, doo"
'Cause the banks are sittin' pretty
And the government's for sale.

But I ain't a gonna tell 'em
"Doo, doo, doo."
That this boat ain't got no oars
"Doo, doo, doo"
'Cause they'll take away my pension
And they'll ship me off to war.

But I won't dance.
"No, he won't dance."
Got ants in my pants.
No, I won't dance.
"He ain't gonna dance."
Got ants inside my pants.
"Doo, doo, doo."

When I'm done singin', ol' Charlemagne starts clappin' like a seal. "*Rah-hah, rah-hah, rah-hah!*" he shouts, like maybe he's at a cricket match. "Stick it to the Hittites!" he jeers. "Stick it to the one-percenters—those cunts who steal your homes and jobs then make you fight their bleedin' wars! *I WON'T DANCE!*" He shouts it out loud. "Let *that* rumble in the cities! Let *that* rumble in the dale! Let it rumble from the top of the song charts! For no longer—*no longer*—will the Hittites be calling the tunes! *Rah-hah, rah-hah!*"

Well, the fucker starts struttin' about while he's speakin' like maybe he's some kind of stud. But that don't fool ol' Pomeroy none. Hell, a flit like that ain't been around pussy since pussy gave him birth. No wonder Pocahontas is drippin' all over the place. No wonder she's ready to jump my bone. So I give Pocahontas the Pomeroy wink and I lift my forefinger to my lips. I let the bitch know that she'll have to wait 'til it's dark and all if she wants some *real* bologna. 'Cause Pomeroy's got class—he don't mount no woman while her boyfriend's lookin' on. No matter how bad she wants it.

AFTER A WEEK OR SO, Charlemagne moves me into his big ol' teepee. He says I'm too great a poet and too great a warrior to be sleepin' out on the grass. So he gives me a cot and a sleepin' bag and tells me to rest up good for the revolution. He even puts me on his payroll—ten dollars a day as long as I keep on singin' *Ants in My Pants*. And let them fuckers keep filmin' me. But when he hands me a ten-dollar bill I just chuckle. Alexander Hamilton—that's who's on it—that founding fucker who said, "The people are a beast." Ain't much else you can say about ol' Hamilton 'cept that he also skipped out on his wife. But that ain't so bad where *that* dude's concerned—at least he had a hard-on for something besides the Electoral College. So I take ol' Charlemagne's money and I thank him for his hospitality. And then I go score me some weed.

Three days later, I get my chance to nail Pocahontas. She's sleepin' in the cot next to mine so I know she'll be mountin' me soon. 'Cause it's four o'clock in the fuckin' mornin' and ol' Charlemagne's out organizin' some rally for later in the day. There ain't nothing to *hold* the bitch back from me now— not unless she trips on her undies while she's rippin' 'em off. So I strip off my shirt, lay back in my cot, and let my pecker rise. 'Cause it won't be much longer 'til the bitch is posin' for a hosin'.

A half hour later, I'm startin' to doze. But I wake up quick when I hear Pocahontas hop out of her cot. It's kinda dark in the tent so she's turned on a flashlight. And *damn* if she ain't got the Jones for my bone: her mouth is all slobbery, her braids are undone, and her hair is spillin' all over her shoulders. And her dark brown eyes are brighter than the flashlight.

"Señor Samson," she whispers, her voice all raw and husky. "Señor Samson, you are *snoring much too loud.*"

She's tryin' to act annoyed, like my snorin' done woke her up, but when I pat her crotch it's me who gets irked. The bitch has a whanger on her that's bigger 'n ol' Pomeroy's. *What kind of shit is this?!*

Now before I can toss the bitch out of the tent— before I can even tell her to haul ass—the flap opens up and Charlemagne pops in. It looks like he's finished up his errand, or maybe this was all a set-up from the start. 'Cause he don't show surprise when he sees me with his bitch—instead he starts jabberin' like he's been vaccinated with a phonograph needle.

"*Rah-hah!*" he shouts. "Remember the Greeks! The chariot of Achilles! The bow of many-wiled Odysseus! Remember the toppling of Troy, the blinding of the Cyclops, and the liberation of sweet, sweet Penelope from a host of loathsome suitors!" As the fucker keeps babblin', his spittle starts flyin' and Pomeroy starts to get damp.

"Why was that?!" he shouts, like I ain't never read *The Iliad*. "Why were the Greeks the most committed of warriors? Why were they such relentless fighters? Why did they so successfully demolish the bastions of greed? *Because*," he hoots, "*they* were the first true anarchists—generous in spirit and selfless in battle! Because they were swift to spot openings and penetrate them! Because they were all for one and one for all! *Rah-hah, rah-hah,* honor the mighty Greeks!"

Well, there ain't no doubt that that fucker wants a three-way so I put on my shirt, grab my guitar, and get my ass out of there *quick*. Ol' Charlemagne may be for sweetness and all, but Pomeroy don't *ride* on the Hershey Highway. So to keep the dude off my tail—to stop him from liberatin' his tallywhacker—I roll that big ol' gas grill into his teepee. Don't matter that the grill's still lit. Don't matter that it's hotter 'n a pistol. Don't matter that it flips over on its side and flames start gobblin' up the canvass. 'Cause if there ain't no *spinners* in that tent—no *real* spinners—there ain't gonna be no *re-vol-u-tion*.

But it looks like I'm gonna get thrown into jail anyhow. 'Cause I can spot 'em through the smoke that's driftin' from the teepee: the biggest army of cops ol' Pomeroy's ever seen. It looks like they've come here to clear out the plaza: there's gotta be two or three hundred of 'em, and they're approachin' the campsites all ramrod straight. Like maybe they got dicks up their asses. And high overhead, this police helicopter is blindin' me with its spotlight. The damn thing's makin' so much racket ol' Pomeroy can't strum his guitar.

Well, it ain't long before the cops start tearin' down tents and puttin' flex cuffs on the protesters. And the protesters ain't puttin' up a *bit* of resistance—some of 'em are even smilin' while the cops are tyin' 'em up. But that all changes when one of the cops spots Pomeroy. The fucker points his baton at me, like he's pointin' to a bomb, then a whole bunch of cops start yellin'.

"There, there, there!"

"A shooter?!"

"Worse! It's that Pomeroy asshole—I know him from Frisco! We locked him up two weeks ago but he got out somehow!"

As the cops close ranks, their voices get even louder.

"He tried to rape Nora—he oughta be in jail!"

"What's he doing now?"

"Burning up evidence!"

"GET HIM, GET HIM, GET HIM!"

"Careful, Careful! The dude's a beast!"

Well, ol' Pomeroy ain't goin' back to jail without no fight. Fuck those Gandhi tactics. So when the cops try to mob me, I grab my guitar by the neck and start swingin'. It ain't exactly the jawbone of an ass, but it damn sure does the trick. I knock down half a dozen of 'em—just like they were bowling pins—and all the while I hear Charlemagne shoutin' through the smoke.

"Just like Davey Crockett!" he cries. "Just like Crockett at the Alamo—knocking down Philistines with the butt of his rifle! Keep swinging, mighty Crockett! Keep swinging! The poets will forever sing your praises!"

Ain't sure why that fucker's still talkin' about swingin', but the cops are what's worryin' me now. With my arms getting tired and Old Betsy in splinters, I ain't got no way to keep fightin' 'em off. But Pomeroy don't need no poets around. Before the cops rap me alongside the head, before they cuff me up and haul me to the meat wagons, I sing 'em three verses of *Ants in My Pants*.

THEY HOUSE ME on J-Range—the disciplinary unit of the Santa Rita Jail. The place ain't much but the acoustics are *real*. Ain't nothin' like steel and stone to amplify a fucker's voice. So I keep on singin' *Ants in My Pants*—all ninety-seven verses—and before I'm halfway done every fucker on the row is bangin' on his cell door and singin', "*Doo doo doo*."

Every fucker but one—this crazy-ass dude who keeps shoutin', "*GOD'S ANGEL WILL GET YOU, SIR!*"

But even the psych nurse—this big-titted bitch who's dispensin' downers—keeps snappin' her fingers and singin', "*Doo, doo, doo*." And she tells me I'm gonna go far. So I'm kinda surprised when the range deputies fetch me out for a visit. Deprive them J-cats of *Pomeroy* and they're gonna start a riot for sure. But that ain't no skin off of Pomeroy's side, so I let

44

the deputies take me through the electronic gate and deliver me to the visitors' row.

Pocahontas—whose visitor's tag reads *Kimberly Foxx*—is waitin' for me behind the partition glass. Bitch can't keep away from me, I guess. And with her fine sculptured body and full pouting lips, she looks just like a statue of Venus. She's clutchin' the phone real tight in her hand—like maybe it's Pomeroy's Willie—but I gotta remember that chick has a dick. So I don't say nothin'—I just sit across from her, hold the receiver to my ear, and let her talk in her deep-ass voice.

She tells me ol' Charlemagne, who ain't in jail yet, just gave me a promotion. He's made me a two-star general. And she says I'm on the Internet now 'cause she filmed me with her iPhone while I was knockin' down them cops. She says Charlemagne's father, a record executive, wants me to cut an album *quick*. While I'm still famous. That means *Ants in My Pants* will soon be climbin' the charts. And she says I'm a hero for settin' the teepee on fire—with smoke blowin' everywhere, them Blac Block anarchists were able to escape the cops. So in a couple of days, Charlemagne is gonna set up a new encampment. It's gonna be east of Frank Ogawa Plaza. Over in Snow Park.

WHEN I'M DONE visitin' with Pocahontas—or whatever the fuck her name is—the deputies take me to the attorneys' module. Got me a *shitload* of charges, I'll bet. But when I see ol' Jessica Jimenez in there, swingin' a sandal from her foot, I kinda forget

45

all that. *Whoooeee*—now there's a *real* woman. The bitch got toes like roasted almonds.

When she sees me, ol' Jessica groans like a hussy and dangles her sandal back onto her foot. And then she looks at me with them hungry eyes of her.

"*Head-ward*," she says to me. "*Shame* on you, Head-ward. *This time* you've gone too far, mi amor."

Well, ol' Pomeroy don't feel like hangin' his head. Not when he's gonna be famous 'n all. But I gotta keep on ol' Jessica's good side if I'm gonna get out of jail. Good thing the bitch has a clit-on for me. So I sit down beside her and give her a big ol' wink.

"How much is too far, Miss Jimenez?" I say.

Well, ol' Jessica acts like she ain't too impressed—like maybe I got somethin' in my eye.

"Head-ward," she snaps. "Must I tell you *everything*? Must I *tell* you not to burn down tents, knock down policemen, or consort with common vandals? Now your behavior is *all over the Internet*. Head-ward, those cockroaches are calling you the Hero of the Alamo."

Ol' Jessica draws herself a deep breath and then starts scoldin' me in Spanish. Don't guess I've ever seen her this mad—even for a Latina, she's pissed. But that ain't nothin' some bologna won't fix. So I thump my chest and scowl like a motherfucker.

"Ain't that a crock of it?" I say. Gotta get her off the rag if I'm gonna score me some make-up sex.

Ol' Jessica just shakes her head. She opens her briefcase slowly, like maybe it's Pandora's box, and she pulls out this pissant newspaper called *The Berkley Slingshot*. On the cover is Pomeroy swingin' Old Betsy. The caption reads *Crockett's Last Stand*.

Well, ol' Jessica's looks like she's ready to swoon, but she keeps on scoldin' me anyhow. "Head-ward, you are also in *Organize, Direct Action, Rolling Thunder*, and about thirty other nasty little rags. I should *box your ears*, Head-ward."

Well, that ain't the box I had in mind, so I tell it to Jessica straight. "Miss Jimenez," I say, "you gotta get me out of here. 'Cause *Ants in My Pants* is gonna go big."

Ol' Jessica don't say nothin' for a while. The way she keeps starin' at that newspaper, you'd think it was a wanted poster. But when she finally speaks to me her voice is kind of soft.

"What are you talking about, Head-ward?" she says. "Are you talking about that vulgar little ditty that somehow got on YouTube? That song about living on sherbet and beating one's carne? How far do you expect that to go, mi amor?"

Well, it sounds like that song has *already* gone big, and that's why ol' Jessica's pissed. Guess she don't want me snatchin' up all that money and glory—not if it means sharin' me with a bunch of groupies. The bitch has her *own* snatch to satisfy. And when she speaks to me again, she makes that *real* clear.

"Mi amor," she says. "You are getting out of jail tomorrow. But not with *my* blessing. If I had *my* way, you'd be locked up for *ten whole years*."

Well, gettin' out of jail sounds good enough to Pomeroy even if Jessica *don't* like it. But I still gotta get the bitch back in my corner. 'Cause I'm gonna need me a business manager when the cash comes pourin' in. Someone I can trust. And there ain't no one I trust more 'n ol' Jessica—even when she's madder 'n a hornet. So I bow my head—just like Oliver Twist—and talk like I'm beggin' her for gruel.

"Seems I'm blessed anyhow, Miss Jimenez," I say.

Ol' Jessica arches her eyebrows—she does that when she wants to make a point—and then she talks to me real gentle.

"Head-ward," she says like she don't want no one to hear her. "Not everyone likes publicity. The mayor, the governor, the police chief himself have asked that your charges be dropped."

Well, I look at ol' Jessica real close—like maybe I'm inspectin' her for lice. And damn if the bitch ain't blushin'.

"Mi amor," she mutters, her voice all throaty now, "you made the Oakland Police Department look very very bad. You made them look like *novicias*."

Well, that gives ol' Pomeroy his biggest charge of all. Maybe this shit *oughta* go to trial. Get me some real press. And some pussy mail too—just like ol' Scott Peterson. That fucker gets three hundred letters a week from women who wanna marry him. Damn good way to lather up the groupies. But there ain't *nothin'* I won't do for ol' Jessica—especially when her tight little butt is on the line. So I nod my head and I grin like a fat cat. 'Cause I don't wanna to show no disappointment.

"Can't be embarrassin' no mayor," I lie.

Ol' Jessica shrugs, reaches into her briefcase, and hands me this official lookin' paper. I don't need to look at it—ol' Pomeroy's seen a hundred stay away orders.

"You're to keep out of Frank Ogawa Plaza," says Jessica. "For *ten whole years. That* is the *deal,* mi amor. And if you want my advice, you'll stay out of Oakland too."

"That ain't no problem, Miss Jimenez," I say. "Ol' Pomeroy follows the wind."

Ol' Jessica arches her eyebrows again, like maybe I went and goosed her. "If you violate the stay away order," she snaps, "I will cuff you up *myself.* The police chief and mayor may have their agenda, but don't expect *me* to sing along with them."

Well, that kinda raises ol' Pomeroy's whanger—the thought of Jessica swingin' a pair of handcuffs. But I sign the order with a big ol' flourish—just like John Hancock would've. And I hand it back to her.

"Gonna give you a break Miss Jimenez," I say.

Jessica takes back the paper and crosses her legs real tight. She's pretendin' she ain't got no drool for my tool.

"Head-ward," she says coolly, "just how do you propose to do that?"

"Gonna make you my manager."

Ol' Jessica rolls her eyes. "I'm *already* your manager," she says.

"Gonna pay you *big* bucks, Miss Jimenez," I say. "Gonna make you so rich you'll be dancin' *La Cucaracha.*"

Ol' Jessica kinda titters—guess the bitch can't help herself. "I suppose," she says, "you're going to buy me a car as well."

"Damn straight," I reply. "Gonna get you a Hummer."

Ol' Jessica sighs and closes up the briefcase. "Head-ward," she says. "I have *never* had a client like you."

IT'S SIX O'CLOCK in the mornin' when they let me out of jail. The sky is eggshell white and the streets are glistenin' everywhere. Like pussies at a Pomeroy concert. And the rain ain't let up yet. So I pull up the hood on my jail-issued sweatshirt and I haul ass to the BART station. By the time I get off at the Oakland City Center, the rain is slackin' up. But the sky is still paler than a motherfucker.

Now ol' Pomeroy's got him a bit of a chill so I blow my nose on the stay away order. The paper ain't *good* for nothin' else—since they cleared all them shitkickers out of the Plaza, it don't make sense to go back there. Not when I'm a two-star general, it don't. And not when I got me an album to cut. So I amble along 20th Street in the direction of Snow Park. Like that fucker who's slouchin' towards Bethlehem.

When I get to Snow Park, I ain't exactly blown away. There ain't no more than forty tents there and the place is crawlin' with homeless dudes. And a couple of the protesters are rakin' up grass for the city. What kind of crap is that?! I ain't sure why they even *call* it Snow Park. Unless they named it after all that speckled bird shit.

Well, it ain't too long 'til this seedy little motherfucker comes runnin' up to me. He's wavin' a black sombrero and he's wearin' a paper badge that says *Occupation Police*. If this is God's angel, ol'

Pomeroy don't have much to worry about. The fucker looks sillier than bat shit.

"Who you be?" he asks. "Who you be? Who you be?" The dude must be watchin' for undercover cops 'cause he's too big an asshole to be one himself.

Well, I just stare at the pissant like I'm about to kick his ass. But suddenly he looks all relieved.

"*Oooooooo*," he says like he just spunked his pants. "You be *Crockett*."

As he runs back to the camp, wavin' his arms and shoutin' "*Woo hoo hoo*," I feel kinda sorry for the dude. When the *real* cops come to clear out the camp, his'll be the first ass they throw in jail. And it won't be long 'til the cops show up—not with all them dispersal notices litterin' the ground.

But this time ol' Pomeroy ain't goin' back to jail. Got me a shitload of fans to take care of. Got me a shitload of money to stash. So I stand behind a tree lookin' down on the park. And I study the place real careful.

Now the sky is gettin' darker, but *that* ain't no surprise. Don't have to be no weatherman to know what's comin' down—ol' Dylan said that before he started sellin' women's panties. And I can see the park real plain. I can see the cops joinin' forces on Harrison Street. I can see the guitar players sittin' by their tents, puffin' weed and strummin' shit. I can see the dudes with Guy Fawkes masks circlin' the lawn with signs that say *We Are Legion*. If them fuckers are legion, I don't know why they call themselves Anonymous.

No, it won't be long 'til the cops sweep the park. But this time they ain't catchin' Pomeroy. Got me too big a contract to sign. Got me too much beaver to bang. So I stay stock-still behind the tree like maybe I been poured outta bronze. But don't be mistakin' me for no statue.

I listen. I watch. And I wait.

2.
Pomeroy &
The Rights of Man

I TOLD YOU HOW I JOINED UP with the Black Bloc Anarchists at Occupy Oakland, those fuckers who wear them Guy Fawkes masks and smash shit up. I told you how the cops raided Frank Ogawa Plaza and how I got put in jail after knocking some of them down with my guitar. I told you how them Blac Block Anarchists loved my music, especially *Ants in My Pants*, and how I ended up on the Internet after knocking down them cops. I even told you how Charlemagne, this English fucker who leads them anarchists, made me a two-star general and told me his father in Manchester was gonna give me a recordin' contract. Don't know if any of that means shit, but what the fuck. Ol' Pomeroy likes to tell stuff.

What I ain't told you is why I'm back in the Santa Rita Jail. How I was arrested again after Jessica Jimenez, my parole officer, sprung me for beatin' up them cops. She told me to keep away from the protest movements, but I ain't back in jail for attendin' no *protest*. I'm back in jail for takin' a piss. For unzippin' my pants in Oakland's Snow Park while police were clearin' out the last of the demonstrators there. This cop came up to me and said, "Oye. Aren't you that Pomeroy asshole? The one who beat up all them cops?" I told him, "I ain't doin' nothin', officer," and I held up my hands to prove it. Well, the cop, he just shook his head and said, "Hanging ten is *not* doing nothing. We call that indecent exposure." I said, "Ten on the slack is *pretty damn decent*," but the cop didn't see the joke. But I didn't make no fuss as he cuffed me up and led me over to the meat wagons. 'Cause they don't keep dudes in jail too long for airin' out their Johnsons. Not in Oakland, they don't.

Well, they got me back on J-Range for now. With all them nut case fuckers. And the craziest of them all is sharin' my cell. He's this skinny little twerp that I know from Frisco—a dude who sells Spanish Fly down in the Tenderloin. I think it's only soda water and egg dye, but the dude sells a *lot* of it. That's why he calls himself Sam the Poontang Man. The fucker *also* knows somethin' about books 'cause he's always quotin' Shakespeare and Rod McKuen. When he ain't jackin' off, that is.

Now there ain't a whole lot to do on J-Range so I go back to singin' *Ants in My Pants*. And them J-cats, they all remember me from the last time I was there. So it ain't long 'til they're chantin' along—singin' "*Doo, doo, doo*" while I'm makin' up new verses. One of the verses goes kinda like this:

Now I'm back inside the pokey
"*Doo, doo, doo*"
But I ain't a stayin' long
"*Doo, doo, doo*"
Cause my groupies wanna grope me

And I got a ten-inch schlong.

But I won't dance.
Got ants in my pants.
No, I won't dance...

Now ol' Sam the Poontang Man ain't chantin' along with 'em. He just starts applaudin' me while I'm singin' and all. But his applause is kinda slow—like maybe he's tryin' to trap himself a fly. And his eyes are so bright that he looks like Charlie Manson.

"Hey, man," he says. "Ya got one minute left."

"A minute left outta what?" I ask him.

"Yer fifteen minutes of fame. That's all them Oakland cops are worth." The dude starts grinnin' like a ghoul, which kinda puts me off my beat. 'Cause his teeth are so crooked he could eat an apple through a picket fence.

"I'm an up-and-comer," I tell him. "Gonna get me a contract with Apple Records."

"You a hit man or something?" the fucker asks me. "That's the only kind of contract yer good for, I'd say."

Well, the dude is startin' to piss me off so I give him the ol' Pomeroy squint. "You sayin' you don't want no encore?" I ask him.

The asshole just looks at me kinda funny. Like maybe I got somethin' in my teeth. "Don't matter a damn what *I* want," he says. "'Cause there *ain't* no second acts. Not in American life anyhow." The fucker starts laughin' and shakin' his head. "So ya may as well be a hit man, dude. Hell, yer built like a brick shithouse."

By now, I'm ready to whip the jerk's ass. But there wouldn't be no challenge to that. So I just glare at him instead. "If there ain't no second acts," I say, "how come I'm back in jail?"

Well, the fucker keeps smirkin' and shakin' his head. "Where else ya gonna get a captive audience, man? Ya got fifteen seconds of *real* fame to go."

Well, I've just about had it with the dude, but I decide to give him another chance. "A chiseler like you got no audience at *all*," I say. 'Less you wanna lather up my groupies for me."

The fucker just keeps laughin', like maybe he's touched in the head.

"It's *you* who's in a lather, man. 'Cause ya know I ain't mouthing no smack."

Before I can lay the fucker out—give him a smack in the mouth—I hear the cell lock jump. A coupla range deputies have come to get me. They're sayin' I got a visitor.

WHEN I GET TO the visiting room, I see Pocahontas waitin' for me. I *told* you about Pocahontas—she's this tranny chick that's Charlemagne's squeeze. But that don't mean she ain't silly for my Willie—my music drives *all* bitches wild. If it weren't for the partition glass, she'd be rippin' the jail-issued pants right off me.

Well, I hold the intercom phone to my ear and I don't say nothin' to her. Don't want the sound of my baritone voice to get her any randier than she already is. So I just sit there and let her do the talkin'.

She tells me Charlemagne and his anarchists are at Cesar Chavez Park in Sacramento. She says they're camped out with the demonstrators there: the students protestin' tuition hikes, the taxpayers protestin' the bank bailouts, and the veterans protestin' the war in Iraq—Bush's colonial war, they call it. She says Charlemagne wants me in Sacramento *quick*. In case the cops start bustin' heads. She says if I beat up a few more cops, Charlemagne will make me a *three-star* general.

Well, I just sit there and keep my lips buttoned. Hell, Pomeroy fought in a colonial war himself. Served two tours in Nam for that Johnson fucker and had me a good ol' time. Pried a fortune in gold from the teeth of dead Cong and dipped *my* Johnson in prime Asian snatch. So it don't hurt a man to be no mercenary. Not if he's greasin' his boom stick, it ain't.

But I don't do nothin' but sit there and grin. 'Cause ol' Pocahontas ain't done talkin' yet. She says *Ants in My Pants* is makin' a splash over in England. She says Charlemagne's father, this big shot at Apple, has already made it into a CD. And it'll score higher ratings than Grateful Dead albums.

When she's finally done talkin', I give Pocahontas a wink. Gonna have me a royalty check to collect. Gonna have me some grateful *groupies* to score. So I tell her I'm gonna be out of jail soon. And I'll see her in Sacramento.

WHEN I'M DONE visitin' Pocahontas, the deputies take me to an attorney room—a room what don't have partition glass. My parole officer is waitin' to see me

57

there—good ol' Jessica Jimenez. I told you about Jessica Jimenez—she's this hot-blooded bitch who oughta be a stripper. 'Cause her tits are bigger 'an grapefruits and her ass is as tight as a drum. And her eyes kinda glow whenever I talk about tacos, tequila, or sex. But Jessica's kinda touchy and all—that's 'cause she's a Latina. And today, she looks like she's got PMS. So I don't say nothin'—I just take a seat and stare at her alligator pumps.

"*Head-ward*," she says to me finally—the bitch likes to use my real name. "*Head-ward Beasley.* I should pistol whip you, señor. Haven't you had enough attention as it is?"

"The attention's just gettin' started," I say. "My groupies are gonna wear my weapon out."

"Is *that* why you took a rest stop, señor?"

Well, I cover my mouth so she don't see me chucklin'. And I look her straight in the eye. "Gonna whip out a pistol myself, Miss Jimenez. It's got a ten-inch barrel."

Ol' Jessica kinda blushes and opens up her field book. Her fingers are thinner 'an asparagus spears. "Just what do you think you *are*?" she mutters. "A *caballo?!*"

Well, there ain't no doubt that the bitch wants my whanger. But ol' Pomeroy needs her for bigger things 'an *that*. "I'm a horse you oughta bet on," I say. "'Cause I want you to be my *manager*."

Ol' Jessica sighs and puts down her field book. Her face looks kinda weary and her breasts are heavin' hard. "Head-ward," she snaps. "How many times do I have to *repeat* this? I'm already your manager."

"Want you to manage my *groupies*," I say. "Want you to count up my cash. I'll make you so rich you'll be dancin' *La Bamba*."

Ol' Jessica smiles, but her smile is pretty thin. Like maybe I insulted her. "Head-ward," she sighs. "I know you're a *wonderful* musician. But is somebody *conning* you, señor? Somebody who wants to take advantage of your brawn?"

Ol' Jessica covers my wrist with her hand. Her palm is cooler 'an an apple, but her lips are glistenin' and hot.

"That's why I want *you* for my manager, Miss Jimenez," I say. "You keep things on the up-and-up."

Now Jessica's startin' to frown so I know she's gettin' pissed at my jokes. And you don't want to be pissin' off a Latina. So I cover my crotch so she don't see my woody and give her a Pomeroy grin. "Gonna give you a stake in my future, Miss Jimenez. Gonna make you a one-percenter."

Well, ol' Jessica, she just keeps glarin'—like maybe I'm talkin' her down. "Mr. Beasley," she snaps. "You need to keep your steak in your *pants*."

"Gonna make you rich, Miss Jimenez," I say. "*That's* what I need to do."

"And why is that, señor?! So I can fiesta and siesta all day?! And drink margaritas?!" *Damn* if the bitch ain't touchy. But instead of slappin' my face, like it looks she's 'bout to do, she places her hands over mine. You never know how a bitch is gonna act. Not when she's starvin' for your Marvin, you don't.

Jessica clutches my hands with her long cool fingers—clutches 'em real tight. And she stares me straight in the eye. "What you *need* to do, mi amor,"

59

she says, "is to stay away from those demonstrators. They're only using you, Head-ward. What you *need* is to get out of Oakland. The policia have your number."

The bitch opens her field book and pulls something out. It's a ferryboat ticket back to San Francisco—a one-way ticket. Her eyes glow like candles as she puts it in my hand.

"We're dropping this charge on you, Head-ward," she says. "Your pistola's not much of a weapon. But if I see you in Oakland again, I will *lock you up myself.* You are much too big for your britches, señor."

THEY LET ME OUT OF JAIL at 8:00 a.m. the next morning. So I head on down to the Oakland Ferry Dock with a couple of anarchists they also let out. And Sam the Poontang Man. For all his jive-ass talkin', the fucker was only serving thirty days on a trespass charge. The dude got himself busted for sleepin' on the steps of Oakland City Hall.

Well, it turns out Sam is an Iraqi vet as well as a bit of a philosopher. It also turns out also that he's scared of cats. Every time one 'em crosses our path, the dude flinches like he been punched.

Finally, I say to him, "What the fuck, dude. For someone in *your* line of business, you don't have much tolerance for pussies."

Well, ol' Sam shakes his head like he's kinda ashamed. "In Bagdad," he says, "cats eat bodies. Don't matter if yer an American or an Arab, man. If you buy the farm in Bagdad, and yer buddies don't scoop you up *quick*, the cats are gonna eat yer body."

"So you kept some fat cats happy," I joke. "Ain't that the reason you went there?"

The dude pinches his nose and blows loose a bugger. "Them fat cats will *never* be happy," he says. "They're stupid-ass dudes trying to snatch up the world—make it their goddamn colony. Fuckers so greedy they see enemies where there ain't none. It's just like it was in Nam there, dude."

"Had me a good time in Nam," I say. "Scored me a whole lot of *Asian* snatch. Shot me a whole lot of gooks."

Ol' Sam shakes his head then spits on the sidewalk. "I was right about you, dude. You *are* a hit man."

"Gonna have me a hit on the charts," I say. "Gonna get me a contract with Apple."

'Ol Sam shakes his head and starts laughin' again. "Whoever told you *that*," he says, "wants you to be their goon."

Well, I've just about decided to whip the dude's ass. But he hands me a roach he's got hid in his pants—a roach he musta snuck outta jail. And then he starts singin' this Dylan song. "*They took a clean-cut kiiid. And they made a killer outta him is what they diiid.*"

For a punk ass hustler, the fucker don't sing bad.

NOW ALL THE WAY to the ferry dock, ol' Sam keeps singin' that song. "*They said what's up is down. They said what isn't is. They put ideas in his head that he thought were his. They took a clean-cut kiiid...*" And them anarchist dudes keep noddin' and clappin' like maybe he wrote that ditty himself. "Right on, dude," they keep sayin'. "Tell it like it is," they keep sayin'. Well, ol' Pomeroy, he just keeps his mouth shut. If the warmongers made a prick outta *Sam*, they didn't have far to go.

As we're walkin' through Jack London Square, ol' Sam stops his singin'. And he starts lookin' around real nervous like. Them anarchists dudes start lookin' 'round too. Turns out Sam and them anarchists have all got stay-away orders from Oakland. And they all got ferryboat tickets to Frisco. They been given twelve hours to get outta Oakland or end up back in the slammer.

Well, there ain't no cops around so Sam lights himself up another roach. And then he looks at the statue of ol' Jack London. "That dude was an oyster pirate," he says. "That dude was a nature faker. And he's got himself a statue."

"You're a bit of a faker yourself," I say. "Sellin' that fizzle water to the tourists. Lettin' 'em think it'll get their wives horny."

Ol' Sam, he just spits and keeps suckin' his roach. "You read Vonnegut, man? You read *Cat's Cradle*?" The fucker don't know that ol' Pomeroy *reads*. That I worked in the library at Quentin. That I've read *Paradise Lost* a dozen times. And Joyce's *Ulysses* a dozen times. So *fuck* Kurt Vonnegut. That's like eatin' a box of Crackerjack when you want yourself a steak.

Ol' Sam makes a gesture with his hands. "Now ya see it. Now ya don't. Cat's Cradle, man—it's a magic trick. That's why I got my own hustle. That's why I stopped fightin' with the Veterans' Administration. *Veterans' benefits*," the dude tosses his roach and spits. "Now ya see 'em. Now ya don't."

Well, ol' Sam starts tellin' me how he ended up in the Army. About how he joined up to get out of jail. About how he killed himself a dozen towel heads so's to beat a punk-ass drug charge. "Man," he says. "They gave me the American Freedom Medal."

Well, now I'm suspectin' that dude's full of shit. 'Cause they don't give no medals to pissants like him. Not big-ass medals, anyhow. Those go to valiant fuckers—the dudes who throw themselves on grenades. And to them hawk politicians who *vote* for them wars—like Hillary Clinton did. Hell, I wouldn't kick ol' Hillary outta bed even if she *does* have thick ankles. Pomeroy *likes* 'em feisty.

By the time we get to the ferry dock, that smart-ass fucker is singin' again. "*Well, it's one, two, three, what are we fightin' faw. Don't ask me, I don't give a damn...*"

"Dude," I tell him, "you *are* full of jive. 'Cause Country Joe was before your time."

Well, the fucker just laughs and hocks himself a loogie. "For a man who's *run* outta time," he says. "You're haulin' some jive yerself. Ya really think you're gonna be a pop star, man?"

"'Ol Pomeroy's in for the *long* haul," I tell him. "I ain't gonna be no flash in the pan."

Well, ol' Sam, he just keeps on laughin'. "'Cept for hangin' out yer Willie," he says. "Ya got no flash at all. Not 'less ya expand something *else*. Yer fifteen minutes of fame, maybe." The dude pulls a bottle of fizzle water from his pants—that shit he's been sellin' to the tourists. He shakes the bottle hard so I can see the water bubblin'. "If yer gonna kick authority in the teeth," he says. "Ya may as well use *both feet*."

Well, by now I'm 'bout ready to brush the fucker off. Tell him to haul ass. 'Cause the only time he opens *his* mouth is to exchange feet. "You think I ain't read Marx?" I ask him.

The fucker starts whoopin' and slappin' his thigh. "Man," he says. "*Keith Richards* said that."

The dude shakes the fizzle water in my face—"Now ya see it," he says. He opens up the bottle and empties it into the channel. "And now ya don't."

AS WE FOLLOW THE COMMUTERS onto the ferryboat, ol' Sam starts hatchin' up a plan. "If ya wanna stay famous," he says, "ya gotta occupy something yerself. Someplace *public*—so you can say you liberated it in the name of the people."

Well, Pomeroy ain't down with *that* kinda shit. Not when the women aboard the ferry are eyein' my bulgin' crotch. 'Cause what needs to be occupied is their pussies. So I tell the dumb ass, "I gone public already. Got my song on the Internet. Gonna have me a contract with Apple."

Ol' Sam, he just snorts and starts waggin' his head. "Cut the crap, man. Ya wanna be another Woody Guthrie? Or some clown who liberated his woody?"

Well, the fucker starts dancin' right there on the poop deck and then he starts singin' this John Lennon song. "*A working class hero is something to beeee...*" Now women are startin' to *eye* him too so the fucker keeps right on singin'. Even after I drag his ass to the sundeck, he keeps on singin' that John Lennon song. "*There's room at the top, they're telling me stiiiiillll. But first ya must learn to smile as you kiiilll...*" And them anarchist fuckers are dancin' along behind him, snappin' their fingers and sayin', "Right on!"

Well, I've just about decided to smash the dude's nose. Don't mind him ravin' and hootin' an' all, but I can't have him jivin' with my groupies. 'Cause that stupid-ass fucker sings pretty damn good.

"Dude," I say finally. "Quit floodin' them pussies with your singin'. That's *Pomeroy* ass you're tryin' to steal."

Well ol' Sam, he starts hootin' all over again. "Open yer eyes, man. Lend me yer ears. Time and tide are calling you, man."

"Ya think I ain't read Shakespeare?" I ask him.

"I don't think ya read him too good," he replies. "'Cause all ya been doin' is *shakin'* yer spear." The dude hocks a loogie over the gunwale and watches it hit the water. "On such a full sea we are now afloat."

"Ain't nothin' to liberate on this ferry," I tell him. "Ain't nothing to occupy *but* pussy."

Well, ol' Sam, he just looks at me kinda profound. Like I'm that Grasshopper dude from *Kung Fu*. "Not if we snatch us the whole fuckin' boat. Hell, man, we could sail it to Sacramento."

"That ain't my kind of snatch," I reply.

"Ya sayin' this boat ain't a public place? Ya sayin' it ain't a taxpayer rip-off?—what with its fucked up schedule and all. Ya sayin' ya don't wanna be on the news again?"

"I'm sayin' I can't score no ass in jail. 'Less I wanna grab me a fairy in *there*."

Well, ol' Sam, he just hocks himself another loogie. "What are they going to do to us, man? I'm a war hero who can't get no *disability* pension. And yer a man of the *people*, dude. At least that's what ya were yesterday." Ol' Sam shakes his head and starts laughin' again. "It ain't just pussy ya grab at the flood. Read yer Shakespeare *again*, man."

Ol' Sam, he starts struttin' around on the sundeck. And he goes back to singin' that punk-ass song. "*Yes, a working class hero is something to beeee. Now ya wanna be a hero, you just follow meeee.*"

DAMN, IF AIN'T EASY to snatch yourself a ferryboat. All I hadda do was barge into the bridge when there weren't no pilots in there. All I hadda do was announce a bomb threat over the PA system—and watch them commuters all chargin' ashore. All I hadda do was fire up the engine while them anarchists cast off the mooring lines. That was pretty damn easy for Pomeroy 'cause I once stole a swift boat in Nam. So before I know it, the four of us—me, Sam, and them anarchist fuckers—are cruisin' down the San Leandro Channel without no care in the world. 'Cept maybe that police helicopter dartin' behind us like a dragonfly.

By the time we putter out into the bay, the seagulls are shriekin' everywhere. 'Cause the harbor patrol is on our ass too. A fleet of punky-ass speedboats skippin' along in our wake. "*CUT YOUR ENGINE!*" a bullhorn keeps blarin'—but ol' Pomeroy don't cut nothin'. Instead, I give ol' Sam the wheel and make my way back to the stern. And there I take me a big ol' piss. Shoot me a stream so golden and tall it looks just like a McDonald's arch. Hell, a good strong piss is better 'an sex. Lasts longer too.

Well, by now we're crusin' past Treasure Island—that man-made mound fulla subsidized housing. We're headin' for the state capitol, says Sam. Gonna join them protesters in Sacramento, he says. And he says we gotta re-name the boat 'cause it now belongs to the people. We can't be callin' it no *Captain Jack*—the name that's stenciled on the bow. So I grab a can of spray paint from one of the anarchists—the paint them dudes use to write *Fuck This Bank*. And after I dangle myself 'longside the bow, I scrawl a new name on the boat. I name it *The Rights of Man*—'cause ol' Pomeroy knows his seafarin' books. Hell, I look just like Queequeg from *Moby Dick*. I wanted to name it *The Pequod,* but I couldn't remember how to spell that.

Well, after I get myself back on the sundeck, ol' Sam starts laughin' like a motherfucker. "Maaan," says the dude like I never *read* Melville. "That's the name of the merchant ship they stole Billy Budd offa. Them British warmongers who wanted to make him into a killer. And when he knocked off an officer who *really needed killing*, they hung him from the mainyard."

Well, ol' Pomeroy, he just starts shakin' his head. Hell, that Billy Budd fucker *deserved* to be hung. If yer gonna frag yerself a gung-ho officer—the kind that'll get your ass killed—ya can't be doin' it in public. Wait 'til the jivester's asleep late at night then toss a pineapple into his hootch. That's how we handled 'em in Nam.

A HALF HOUR LATER, we're passin' San Quentin and enterin' the San Pablo Bay. And them anarchist farts are struttin' about on the sundeck. The dudes are wearin' their Guy Fawkes masks and shootin' the bird at the harbor patrol boats. And ol' Sam gets ahold of the spray paint can and writes *Dude, Where's My Country?* on the sundeck. That's so the news helicopter hoverin' above us can see that we got us a *message*. Bet he stole that phrase from Michael Moore, that prick who makes fuck you movies. If ol' Sam ain't more careful 'an *that*, he's gonna get sued for *plagiarism*.

Well, ol' Sam, he radios the harbor patrol while I keep on steerin' the boat. He tells 'em we're on a mission. He tells 'em we took back a piece of the country. Liberated it in the name of the people. Ain't sure that includes them commuter-ass fuckers, but what the hell. 'Cause the sun is shinin', the bay is glitterin', and whitecaps are boilin' like twats. Ol' Pomeroy's havin' a good ol' time.

An hour later, while I'm steerin' the tub past Point Pinole, ol' Sam turns the radio on full blast. And damn if we ain't on the national news. This broadcaster bitch, who sounds like Barbara Walters, is sayin a buncha vandals have stole the San Francisco Bay Ferry. She's sayin' they wired it up with explosives and that seafarin' craft had better beware. Guess the harbor patrol musta spoke to that bitch. Hell, they're cruisin' a half mile behind us now 'cause they don't wanna get blown up.

But the bitch don't mention ol' Pomeroy at all, and that kinda pisses me off. Ain't no sense in being a man of the people if that don't sell you no albums. But if a fucker don't ring his own bell, ain't nobody else gonna do it. So I give ol' Sam the wheel and I grab me the can of spray paint. And I hang from the bridge with only one hand—just like Quasimodo, the hunchback of

Notre Dame, mighta done. And I write *ANTS IN MY PANTS* right across the bulwark. So folks'll know *Pomeroy's* aboard.

Well, ol' Sam ain't a fucker to be outdone. 'Cause after I slide on down from the bulwark, I notice him out on the sundeck. He's got the PA mic on an extension cord and he's singin' *Wake Up Little Susie* in this big ass voice. 'Cept that he's changed the words around some. But his voice is so loud they gotta be hearin' him halfway to Sacramento.

Well, ya'll fell sound asleep.
Wake up little Susie and weep.
The game is over, it's four o'clock.
And yer in trouble deep.
Wake up, little Suuuusie.

And them anarchist fuckers are dancin' behind him and singin' out, "*Ooo La La.*"

I AIN'T TOLD YOU yet how we came to the mouth of the Sacramento River. How we bobbed about first in the Carquinez Strait 'cause the tide looked kinda low. How we sunk anchor 'til the following morning and waited for a full sea. One we could take at the flood. And how them police helicopters kept buggin' us all night long. With their goddamn flutterin' overhead, ol' Pomeroy couldn't sleep for shit.

Well, ol' Sam turns the radio on full blast when we're finally cruisin' the Strait. And that broadcaster bitch is *still* runnin' us down. She's tellin' the whole damn country how we're nothin' but a pack of thieves. How we're pretendin' to be like Robin Hood so's we could steal ourselves a boat. The way she keeps runnin' her mouth and all, she's gotta be achin' for a snakin'.

Well, soon we're passin' Semple Point and headin' on under the Carquinez Bridge. And the whole damn bridge is packed with people, all standin' shoulder to shoulder. They're holdin' up signs that say, *Where's Our Country?* And they're cheerin' us like motherfuckers. So I cut the engine and ease the boat dockside so's we can let a few of 'em aboard. And before I know it, *The Rights of Man* is packed with patriots. There's Tea Party fuckers and NRA dudes an' they're bringin' us a keg of beer. There's horny bitches with *God Hates Gays* buttons who're given' ol' Pomeroy the eye. There's Christian Coalitioners with anti-abortion pins and fuckers with buttons that say *Close Our Borders*. There's even a raincoat wearin' dude whose pockets are burstin' with candy—case we all get hungry. By the time we're headin' back on up the Strait, we got us a goddamn freedom boat.

An hour later, I swing the boat portside and steer it up the Sacramento River. And half them fuckers are blind drunk. That's when ol' Sam and me decide to have us a concert. So we rig up the PA system on the sundeck while them anarchist dudes steer the boat. And then I start singin' out *Ants in My Pants*. And before I know it, the whole damn boat's singin' *"Doo, doo, doo."*

Well, they sold us up the river
"Doo, doo, doo."
But we grabbed ourselves the boat.
"Doo, doo, doo."
So no matter what they figger

We're a gonna stay afloat.

Yes we're havin' us a party
"Doo, doo, doo."
That we never will forget.
"Doo, doo, doo."
Everybody's hale and hearty.
And the twats are soppin' wet.

Now ol' Sam, he starts jitterbuggin' while I'm beltin' out the chorus. And then he starts makin' these boogy woogy sounds. And before I know it, everyone aboard is cheerin' like it's the Fourth of July.

Well, I won't dance.
"Boogaldy boo hoo hoo"
Got ants in my pants.
"Scobaldy scoo woo hoo"
No, I won't dance.
"Hubba, hubba, bubba hey".
Got ants inside my pants.
"Hoy, hoy, hoy, hoy."

Next thing I know, ol' Sam snatches the mic right outta my hand and starts singin' his *own* damn verses. And the crowd keeps on singin' out, *"Doo, doo, doo."* Drunk as them fuckers are, they probably don't even know what they're listenin' to. But that don't stop 'em from hollerin' along while Sam keeps singin' his shit.

Well, they sent me to the boonies
"Doo, doo, doo"
Where I hadda kill and toil

"Doo, doo, doo"
'Cause our leaders all are loony
And they wanna steal the oil.

But we're gonna kill their fables
"Doo, doo, doo"
Gonna put 'em in the ground
"Doo, doo, doo"
Fuck the women if yer able
'Cause we're Sacramento bound.

And that's what we were doin'—latherin' up the twats and singin' like shit—when those anarchists ran us aground.

I AIN'T YET MENTIONED how the sound system died after the hull made a noise like an elephant screechin'. How we sat on a sandbar twenty miles south of Sacramento and couldn't hook nothing back up. I ain't told you how I gunned the engine like a motherfucker 'cause the boat wouldn't move for shit. And how them horny-ass bitches aboard all wanted to keep on partying. So I hadda sing them broads *Ants in Your Pants* without no fuckin' mic.

Now half an hour later, this fleet of flatboats pulls alongside us—boats that are jack full of cops. There's maybe fifty or sixty of the fuckers—all of 'em soaked to the skin. And before ol' Pomeroy can sing the next chorus, them drippin'-ass fuckers are swarmin' onto the deck. They musta figured we didn't have no bomb—not with all them sunshine patriots aboard.

Well, it ain't no big surprise when ol' Jessica climbs aboard too. Guess she musta spotted me on the news.

Guess she couldn't keep away from no Pomeroy concert. 'Cause I ain't never seen her more pumped for my stump: her tight ass dress is clingin' wet and her thin pointy heels look sharper 'an weapons. And the bitch looks ready to rip them heels off and start swingin' 'em at the groupies.

Well, the cops, they start grabbin' folks left an' right an' frog marchin' 'em to the flatboats. But the trouble don't come to a head 'til Jessica snatches my wrist. 'Til she slaps a handcuff over it and starts pleadin' to me in Spanish. "*Ay, mi caballo*," she cries. "*Ay, mi amor. Yo te quiero, yo te quiero, yo te quiero.*" At least, that's what I think she says.

Well, them Tea Party dudes, they start growlin' at ol' Jessica. 'Cause they don't want no Mexicans tellin' folks what to do. And when one of 'em calls Jessica a wetback whore, that's when things come to a boil. It ain't long after that 'til all hell breaks loose—'til folks start shovin' back at the cops and the cops start crackin' skulls. And that raincoat wearin' fucker, he's singin' "*Yank me doodle*" and peltin' everyone with candy. Damn, if it don't get crazy as hell.

Now the deck is so packed with elbows and assholes there ain't much room to move. But the cops grab Sam the Poontang Man anyhow. And then they start passin' him overhead, like the crowd does with Garth Brooks at one of his concerts. And ol' Sam he keeps on singin' as the cops keep passin' him along. He's singin' *Wake Up Little Susie* again. And he's singin' it like a motherfucker.

Well, yer movie wasn't so hot.
It didn't have too good a plot.

73

Ya fell asleep. Yer goose is cooked.
Yer reputation is shot.
Wake up little Suuusie.

And long after they pass ol' Sam over the gunwale—
long after they rev up a flatboat to hustle his butt
ashore—I hear his big ass voice.

I AIN'T YET SAID how I pulled me a Quasimodo.
How I saved ol' Jessica from them Tea Party fuckers
after she kicked one of 'em in the groin. 'Cause when
that drunk-ass fucker started rubbin' his balls,
demandin' she make an apology, the rest of them
dudes start shovin' her back and forth. An' accusin' her
of swipin' an American job.

Well, by now ol' Pomeroy's tired of them fuckers.
Hell, that's prime-ass pussy they're messin' with. So I
grip me the handcuff chain, the one still danglin' from
my wrist, and start swingin' the loose handcuff at their
heads. And after I brain two or three of 'em, I grab ol'
Jessica and toss her over my shoulder. Just like ol'
Quasi done with Esmeralda—that Gypsy spinner the
church was gonna hang.

Well, ol' Jessica, she starts cussin' like a Spaniard
and tellin' me to put her down. She keeps callin' me
puerco an' *imbécil* and a lotta other Spanish names.
And damn if that don't hurt ol' Pomeroy's feelings.
'Cause Latinas ain't shy about cussin' you out—
especially when they're achin' for your bacon. So ol'
Pomeroy hops on over the gunwale with Jessica still on
his back. And then I drop her in waist deep water. Hell,
the bitch could use a drenchin' just to cool her crotch.

Well, ain't nobody payin' attention to us as I hustle ol' Jessica ashore. 'Cause *The Rights of Man* is startin' to sway from all them fuckers on it. And it looks like the prow's got a big ol' crack and will soon be suckin' in water. But ol' Jessica don't give a shit about the boat— she just keeps on mutterin' in Spanish as I follow her ass ashore. Then she plops herself down on a sandbank and starts to rub her feet.

"Head-ward," she murmurs, her voice all feathery now. "Head-ward, I've lost my shoes."

She's wigglin' her toes in the sand while she's talkin', and the soles of her feet are all cut up. But I crack me a woody anyhow and I give her a big ol' wink.

"Ya gotta be my manager now," I tell her.

Ol' Jessica, she just starts shakin' her head like maybe I'm talkin' trash. "Mr. Beasley," she says, her voice now cooler 'an ice. "Are you *completely* loco, señor? Why on earth do I *have* to be your manager?"

"That's why I saved your butt," I say. "That's why I saved ya like ol' Quasimodo."

Ol' Jessica don't say nothin' for awhile. She just keeps starin' out on the river—starin' at *The Rights of Man*. And damn if that tub don't look ready to sink. "Mr. Beasley," she says to me finally. "Must *everything* be a fantasy to you?"

"A fantasy saved your ass," I say. "And *you* got an ass worth savin'."

Well, ol' Jessica buries her face in her hands. Like maybe she don't wanna see me no more. But when she lowers her hands, her eyes are bright with lust.

"Get out of here, Head-ward," she hisses. "Get out of here *now—vaya*. I've had *enough* of your caca for one day."

Well, I guess the bitch don't trust herself, but there ain't time to screw her anyhow. 'Cause when the cops finish bustin' them patriot assholes, they're gonna come after ol' Pomeroy. So I pick me the handcuff lock with this nail that's lyin' in the sand. And I hand the cuffs back to ol' Jessica. Don't want the bitch to get in no trouble for losin' state-issued equipment.

Well, it ain't too far to Route 84, which is a straight shot to Sacramento. So ol' Pomeroy, he takes off at a trot. 'Cause I got me more verses to sing. I got me more beaver to bang. An' I got me a check to collect.

3.
Pomeroy &
The New World Order

GONNA SEE BIG BEN and them beef beater guards. Gonna sample me some of that English cuisine. And shag me a few of them birds. That's what they call spinners over there—birds. Which is kinda appropriate when you think about it. 'Cause when they get a dose of ol' Pomeroy, they're gonna be shriekin' like starlings.

Now I'm also goin' to London to sign my contract with Apple Records. That's why that Charlemagne fucker sent me an airline ticket. He says I gotta get there quick if I wanna be as famous as The Beatles. Time and tide wait for no man, he says. And if I beat up a few of them bobbies for him, he'll make me a *three star general.*

Since I been to prison an' all, I decide to get a letter from my parole officer. A letter sayin' I'm off parole and my ass has been rehabilitated. In case some fucker in airport security tries to take away the passport I just got. And report ol' Pomeroy to Homeland Security. So

I phone Jessica Jimenez at the San Francisco Parole Office and ask her to write me a letter. Even though I'm off parole, I still drop in on the bitch now an' then. 'Cause after I carried her offa that ferry, ol' Jessica done me a favor. She told the police it was Sam the Poontang Man what masterminded that ferryboat heist. She told 'em ol' Pomeroy was workin' undercover so the cops could bust that fucker. But the DA didn't press no charges on Sam. 'Cause the dude's an Iraqi war vet who dusted some towel heads for the government. And he can't get no disability pension even though he's mad as a hatter.

Now since ol' Jessica done me a favor, I'm gonna make her rich. Gonna talk her into being my manager so she don't have to mess with parolees no more. 'Cause some of them fuckers are crazy and I don't want the bitch gettin' hurt. Can't have ol' Jessica gettin' beat up—her tits are too damn fine.

Well, I'm sittin' in Jessica's office on Mission Street, tryin' to hide my woody with my hands, when she looks at me with them smolderin' eyes of hers. The bitch looks ready to fall to her knees and whip out ol' *Pomeroy's* Big Ben.

"Head-ward," she says to me finally, her voice all smoky and raw. "*Why* do you keep insisting I be your manager? I'm not even in charge of you anymore."

"Ya done me a solid, Miss Jimenez," I say. "And Pomeroy takes care of his own."

Ol' Jessica, she just shakes her head and shuffles herself some papers. She don't get mad at them jokes no more, not since I got myself off parole. All she does now is give me food vouchers and tell me I'm full of shit.

When the bitch is done shufflin', she picks up a pencil. Like maybe she needs to occupy her hands so she won't be grabbin' my crotch. But I can't be screwin' her anyhow—ol' Jessica don't wanna share. A dude can't have no *groupies* if he's humpin' himself a Latina.

Well, Jessica starts nibblin' the nub of her pencil like maybe it's Pomeroy's schlong. And then she looks me straight in the eye. "Head-ward," she says. "I have written you that letter. You're no longer a ward of the state, señor—you can go wherever you want. But what on earth do you know about England?"

Ol' Pomeroy just sits there and grins like a fat cat. Hell, I seen every episode of *Upstairs Downstairs* when I was workin' in the Library at San Quentin. So I know all about them ladies and lords and how ya gotta talk to a butler. Gonna *buy* me one of them English mansions when I've made me a million or two. And once I'm as famous as The Beatles, I'm gonna shag Penny Lane.

"Gonna get myself knighted, Miss Jimenez," I say. "Like ol' Mick Jagger done."

Ol' Jessica kinda sighs, but Pomeroy's got a point. If Mick Jagger can get himself knighted—just for screamin' and wavin' his arms around—then any ol' fucker can do it. Even if he's been to prison.

I notice ol' Jessica's shakin' her foot like maybe her pump is too tight. Whenever the bitch is fed up with ol' Pomeroy, she starts to shake her foot. "Mr. Beasley," she says, her voice all suspicious now. "Just why did that *culo* send you an airline ticket?"

"'Cause I'm gonna sign me a contract," I say.

"A contract to do what? Are you going to put on a diablo mask and beat up policemen again?"

"Gonna beat off some groupies is all," I tell her. "Don't need no mask for that."

Well, the bitch just sits there and looks at her nails. Like maybe she's washin' her hands of ol' Pomeroy. "Why do you want to be rich?" she asks me. "You seem very happy to sponge off the city and sing your ditties on the street. Head-ward, you never even change your pantalones."

"Gonna make you wealthy too, Miss Jimenez—just like them one-percenters. And then you can fiesta and siesta all day and bust yourself some piñatas."

Ol' Jessica frowns and her nostrils start flarin'. That's how she gets when I'm pissin' her off. "Mi amor," she snaps. "You're lucky I didn't bust *you*."

"It's them anarchists what need bustin'," I say. "'Cause I can't sing for shit when they're hollerin' and all."

Ol' Jessica, she starts rollin' her eyes like maybe her contacts are hurtin'. "They want you to dance to *their* tune, Head-ward. They want to take advantage of your brawn. Can't you *see* that, mi amor."

"Gonna have me a dance with the Queen, Miss Jimenez. And shoot me some quail with Prince Charles."

Ol' Jessica just keeps shakin' her foot. "Really, Head-ward. And what *else* are you going to do?"

"I'm gonna see Piccadilly Circus," I say. "And throw me some peanuts at the elephants."

Ol' Jessica, she don't say anything more. She just opens her desk drawer and reaches inside. Then she gives me the letter for my trip.

I PICK UP TWO GENERAL ASSISTANCE CHECKS on the same day my flight's gonna leave. So I cash the checks quick at the Wells Fargo Bank on Market Street. I collect my money—all four hundred dollars—in hundred dollar bills. Benjamins I call 'em 'cause that's who's on 'em—that kite-flying fucker who went to France and balled more bitches 'an Pomeroy. Then I catch me a cab to the San Francisco International Airport. 'Cause I ain't got time for no slow-ass subway—not when I'm goin' abroad like ol' Ben.

When I get to the airport, the cab driver gives me a second look. Seems he ain't sure I can pay him no forty dollar fare. So I slip him one of them Benjamins and tell him to keep the change. Now that I'm gonna be famous an' all, I gotta start tippin' big.

Well, the airport's so fulla soldiers that it's hard to move around. Guess them dudes are headin' to Afghanistan—or maybe they're comin' back. And there's towel heads struttin' all over the place, like they own a big piece of the country. Like Obama done traded it to 'em for their oil. But that ain't no skin offa Pomeroy's side—I'm still gonna rake in the cash. 'Cause them towel heads don't know what their women are *for*—they dress 'em like nuns. Hell, them bitches are gonna be gushin' like oil wells when Pomeroy gets himself famous.

When I'm halfway through the security checkpoint, I'm already gettin' the eye. A coupla Muslim women are standin' in line behind me. And they're watchin' me with cock-starved eyes like they don't wanna stay in no harems owned by fuckers named Abdul. Not

81

after seein' the bulge in ol' Pomeroy's pants. But I
don't say nothin' after I clear the checkpoint—I just
grab up my guitar and my Army surplus rucksack. And
then I haul ass *quick*. Hell, them bitches look ready to
rip off their burqas and fight for ol' Pomeroy's schlong.
And Pomeroy don't mess with another man's harem.

After I find me my terminal, I sit down and wait
for my flight. And while I'm waitin', I unpack my guitar
and strum it like a motherfucker. It's harder to tune
than ol' Betsy, the guitar I smashed on the heads of
them cops, but it soaps up the twats just the same. So I
compose some new verses to *Ants in My Pants* and I
sing 'em like Willie Nelson.

> *Well, I'm off to jolly England.*
> *Gonna fly from shore to shore.*
> *Gonna show them Limey strumpets*
> *What they never seen before.*
>
> *And when I've given 'em their jollies*
> *And the shaggin' of their dreams*
> *Gonna catch myself a trolley*
> *And have crumpets with the Queen.*

Now before I can sing out the chorus, this
redheaded counter attendant leans over me. And she
starts speakin' to me in this twangy Aussie accent.
"You a veteran, Clyde?" she snaps. She's starin' at my
military rucksack like maybe it's got a bomb in it.

The bitch looks kinda old to be on the rag, but ol'
Pomeroy's gotta be careful. Ya don't wanna piss off no
redhead if her hormones are outta whack. So I answer
her in a soft-ass voice.

"Served two tours in Nam." I tell her. "Shot me a big ol' mortar."

The bitch wrinkles her nose then she draws a deep breath. Like she's plannin' to blow a didgeridoo. "A lot of veterans are flying these days," she says. "And we're happy to have them on Virgin Atlantic. But usually they fly standby on the military flights."

I give the broad the ol' Pomeroy wink, but I don't feel no juice in my spruce. 'Cause her tits look kinda dried-up and her hair looks kinda dyed. And Pomeroy don't screw prune twats.

"Fuck flying standby," I say to her. "That's like stirrin' sloppy seconds."

Well, the bitch kinda gasps and starts waggin' her head. And she looks at me with these wide-ass eyes. "You trying to be a rock star, Clyde? You seem a bit old for that."

"Gonna be bigger 'an Jagger," I tell her. "Ol' Pomeroy sings from the heart."

The bitch bites her lip then starts lookin' around. "Sir, we're happy you're on the flight. But please put away that guitar."

"Ol' Pomeroy fought for our freedoms," I tell her. "That's why I went to Nam."

The bitch shakes her head like she knows I'm talkin' trash. Hell, Pomeroy didn't free nothin' in Nam—nothin' but his Willie. But it don't hurt a veteran to raise the ol' flag now and then. Damn good way to score beer and pussy. As long as you don't tell folks more 'an they wanna hear.

"Sir," says the bitch, her voice sharp as a tack, "please put away that guitar."

"Fought for ol' Glory," I tell her. "Fought for motherhood and apple pie."

The bitch squares her shoulders and glares at ol' Pomeroy. "*Sir*," she says, "*put away your guitar. People don't want to hear you sing.*"

She looks about ready to phone security, and I don't wanna miss my flight. So I shove the guitar back into its case. And I give her my boarding pass.

WHILE I'M BUCKLED into my seat, waitin' for that big ol' Boeing to take off, a coupla passengers thank me for my military service. That's like thankin' a hooker for spreadin' the clap, but ol' Pomeroy just gives 'em a smile. At least I scored me some pussy in Nam. At least I had me some fun. In *Afghanistan*, a dude can't even *wet* his whanger. Even though them towel heads can't fuck. Even though their women are hard-up. Hell, a woman ain't cum in Afghanistan since 1492.

Well, there ain't a whole lot to do on that jet, so I look at this pamphlet ol' Charlemagne sent me. The dude's real name is Brian Hines, but he uses the name of that Renaissance fucker. Now Brian ain't no sword-wieldin' king, but the dude can write his ass off. That's 'cause he's been to Oxford and has a degree in the classics. So while we're taxiing down the runway, I read that pamphlet again.

April 20, 2014
A Message from the People's Movement
Who among you would a debt slave be? If so, speak up for you we have offended. Who among you

would have your e-mail intercepted by the Government Communication Headquarters? If so, speak up for you we have offended. Who among you would be made impotent by chemically altered foods? If so, speak up for you we have offended.

Those who are not offended, those with the blood of Guy Fawkes in their veins, are invited to join the People's March on May 1, 2014. On that day, all true patriots will march from Clerkenwell to Trafalgar Square. On that day, the rage of the people will crash like a tsunami upon the pillars of greed and avarice. On that day, the one-percenters will tremble in their stolen mansions and rue their politics of deceit, murder, and subjugation.

Know that we are Anonymous. Know that we are legion. And know that we are joined by the mightiest 99-percenter of all. Some call him Samson because he brained forty Philistines with the jawbone of an ass. Some call him Crockett because he shattered Old Betsy upon the skulls of the centurions. Some call him Pomeroy, a street name he uses to thwart the spooks of the National Security Agency. But by whatever name he's given, he is the very embodiment of John Adams and Benjamin Franklin, men who warned us that oligarchs steal republics.

No longer will we be crushed by the heel of the New World Order. No longer will we be duped by Barack Obama and his flunkies in British Parliament. No longer will we sail obediently to our doom like the ill-fated crew of The Pequod. On May Day, our voices will rise loud and clear.

I guess ol' Charlemagne's still full of shit, but it don't bother Pomeroy none. 'Cause I don't mind bein' a man of the people—not if it'll help me sell albums and score pussy. But I can't sing my songs on no candy-ass jet—not without being arrested by some air marshal. So after I've had me a snack, I punch up an in-flight movie. It's a lame-ass flick called *Lost in Translation*.

WHEN I GET TO HEATHROW AIRPORT, I head for the passport gate quick. 'Cause some Muslim women are followin' me—spooky looking bitches in burqas and veils. And Pomeroy ain't mountin' no bitch he can't see. But it ain't much improvement when I get past the gate and see Pocahontas waitin' for me. I told you about Pocahontas—she's this fudge-packin' chick who had Pomeroy fooled 'til I grabbed me some of her crotch. The bitch may look like an Indian maiden, but her schlong is as long as a donkey's. And Pomeroy don't fuck trannies.

Well, Pocahontas, she tells me the May Day March is on. She says ten thousand marchers are rallying in Trafalgar Square: union folks, students, and tree huggin' fuckers. She says they're protestin' apartheid. She says they're protestin' empire. She says they're protestin' the drone strikes in Afghanistan. She also says Charlemagne just got himself busted—that's why he ain't at the airport. 'Cause the fucker threw chicken blood on a coupla English cops. And called 'em Gestapo pigs. And after the cops threw his ass in jail, they snatched that pamphlet with Pomeroy in it. Pocahontas says the cops wanna bust me too 'cause they don't want me stirrin' up the unions. She says I was lucky to get through customs and I gotta leave

London quick. And she hands me this bus ticket to Ireland.

I follow Pocahontas down this long-ass subway tunnel and we hop on the London Tube. And we get out at Piccadilly Circus 'cause I wanna turn my money into pounds. And maybe see some elephants. But as soon as we leave the subway station, I know I done made a mistake. Hell, the street is so crowded with union-ass marchers, I can't even find me a bank. There's fuckers blowin' whistles. There's fuckers poundin' drums. There's fuckers with signs that read, *Stop the Cuts* and *Vote Socialist*. Don't know what the fuck votin' socialist means. If votin' made a difference, folks wouldn't be allowed to do it.

Now except for the fish shops and double-decker buses, ol' London seems kinda like Oakland. I even see the cops lookin' over the crowd like they're tryin' to spot ol' Pomeroy. So as soon as I see me a money exchange, I duck through the doorway quick. And I trade my Benjamins for a buncha Lizzies. That Limey money got Liz all over it—back when she was a piece of ass. And once I got my money, I follow Pocahontas to Victoria Station.

Well, there ain't no cops in Victoria Station so I whip out the ol' guitar. And then I start singin' like Johnny Cash.

Well, I'm off to bonny Ireland
Gonna see the emerald isle.
'Cause them Irish eyes are smilin'
And I won't get thrown in jail.

And before I know it, I'm sittin' alone in the back of this big-ass bus. And I'm headin' for the land of the leprechauns.

TURNS OUT OL' POMEROY'S ridin' on a tour bus. And the bus is fulla dowager bitches with punk-ass bladders. 'Cause the driver keeps stoppin' every fuckin' hour to let them bitches piss. So Pomeroy, he takes himself a long-ass nap. And when I wake up, we done crossed the Irish Sea on a ferryboat. And we're parked at the castle of some feudal-ass chieftain.

"*Blarney Castle*," the driver calls out and Pomeroy takes himself a look. Guess they call it that 'cause the owner was fulla bull. But that don't mean shit when you're a feudal fucker. Ya still get to drink mead all day. Ya still get to attack other fiefdoms. And ya still get to fuck any woman ya want. And ya don't need no NSA to keep folks in line. If a fucker starts talkin' smack to ya, ya just gotta chop off his head.

Well, ol' Pomeroy decides to kiss the Blarney Stone. Get me the gift of gab, as they say. 'Cause I need some new verses to *Ants in My Pants*—I only got a hundred and fifty-two of 'em. Gonna need more 'an that if I'm gonna stay famous. So I walk on past this giant dungeon that looks like Batman's cave. Damn good place to torture fuckers that won't stop talkin' smack. And once I find my way into the castle, I walk up these narrow stairs. And I find me this deep-ass pit where they got the Blarney Stone hid.

Now kissin' that stone kinda pisses me off. First, I gotta stand in line with some tourist hussies who oughta be kissin' ol' Pomeroy's stones. And then I gotta bend over backwards like some limbo-dancin' dude. And listen to some bossy fucker tellin' me to keep the line movin'. It ain't worth the trouble, if ya ask ol' Pomeroy. So after I kiss that grainy-ass stone, I head on back down the stairs.

As soon as I get my butt out of that castle, I see some old geezer laughin'. He's sittin' on a bench, holding his sides, and laughin' like a goddamn banshee. He's laughin' so hard he can't hardly draw breath to speak. "Oh my," he says. "Me lad, me lad. Locals pee on that stone, you know?"

Now *that* riles Pomeroy up for sure. So I unzip my pants, whip out ten of the finest, and take me a piss of my own. Right on the side of that jive-ass castle. Shoot me a stream so goddamn tall that it's throwin' off a rainbow. And that rainbow don't even *start* to fade 'til my pecker is back in my pants.

It ain't long after that 'til some frog-face fucker comes runnin' up to me. A loud little dude with a whiskey-red nose and a security badge on his chest. And the dude keeps yellin' in this squeaky-ass voice. "Your pee don't *belong* on our castle, guv. What you think you're doing, hey?"

"Spendin' a penny," I say. "Ya want me to give you change?"

The dude don't even answer Pomeroy—he just starts shoutin' into a hand radio. Repeatin' some kinda code. Didn't know they *had* no code for pissin' on mossy-ass rocks. Then he looks at me with this Clint Eastwood squint. "You that Yank they call Pomeroy?" he says finally. "The bloke who beats up cops? I saw you once on the news, I think."

"Gonna be more famous 'an that," I tell him. "Ya want ol' Pomeroy's autograph?"

Well, the dude lifts the radio close to his mouth, like he's plannin' to give it a smooch. "Yes, yes," he keeps mutterin' all impatient-like. "Calls hisself Pomeroy, but that may be an alias. And he looks like a South Sea islander." When the fucker's done listenin', he lowers the radio and sticks out his scrawny chest. "Guv," he says, "you're famous enough already."

"What you mean by that?" I say.

"You got a police record, guv—fifty bleedin' arrests. You're on a watch list of political undesirables. Who allowed you into this country, hey? Some bleedin' heart liberal write you a hall pass?"

Damn if ol' Pomeroy don't shake his head. Hell, a fucker don't get tagged quick as that 'less he's pissed off the New World Order. And his record has jumped to the top of the charts.

Well, it looks like I gotta get outta there quick. So I run on back to the tour bus and grab my rucksack and guitar. And after I find me a road with some signs, I trot in the direction of Cork.

WHEN I GET TO CORK CITY, it's almost dark. And ol' Pomeroy ain't too impressed. It's a jive-ass little town fulla churches and pubs and old-ass architecture. But ol' Pomeroy's ready to soak in some culture. So I find the town square, buy me some fish an' chips, and grab me this skinny little newspaper called *The Corkman*. And damn if ol' Pomeroy ain't in *The Corkman*. The article don't say nothin' 'bout *Ants in My Pants* or how I'm gonna be on tour. It just says some transient bum done pissed on Blarney Castle. And he oughta be hunted down and jailed for desecrating a shrine.

Well, that paper's also talkin' 'bout Edward Snowden, that tattlin' dude Obama wants to bust. 'Cause that fucker told every swingin' dick in the world how Obama's been interceptin' e-mail. Just like Joseph Stalin done. Now that makes Pomeroy madder 'an shit. Ol' Snowden ain't even cut himself an album and he's got three pages of press. So I call up Pocahontas on this cell phone she done gave me. And I tell her some whistle-tootin' fucker is gettin' more publicity 'an Pomeroy.

Pocahontas, she tells me to keep my pecker up. 'Cause the New World Order controls the newspapers. And the New World Order controls the politicians. And the New World Order wants to *smear* ol' Pomeroy, not make him a goddamn star. She says I gotta keep singin' my songs so's to drown them one-percenters out. 'Cause Charlemagne's still locked up and government goons are everywhere. They're roundin' up anarchists left and right. And puttin' 'em in jail with IRA fuckers and whacked-out soldiers back from Iraq. She says Obama ain't no better than that feudal fucker whose castle I pissed on.

When I'm done talkin' with Pocahontas, I look around for cops. Then I crack me a big ol' stiffy. 'Cause some hot Irish babe is ooglin' me from across the square—an earth mother type with natural red hair and tits that are bigger 'an grapefruits. A bitch like that *deserves* to be fucked. And no one fucks better 'an a redhead. So I whip me out the ol' guitar and make up more verses to *Ants in My Pants*.

I'm a hero of the people
And I got Obama foiled
'Cause he 's got no use for fuckers
That he can't sell out for oil.

So he's roused the New World Order
And he's put 'em on my trail
But I'm gonna play my music
And I'm gonna score some tail.

Now it ain't too long 'til ol' Pomeroy's drawn himself a crowd. Folks are standin' all around me, clappin' their hands and singin', *Rig un du rum da* while I'm beltin' out the verses. 'Til some wild-eyed asshole with a bushy beard points his finger right at me. "*You're the one*," he shouts. "*You're the bloke wot tinkled on Blarney Castle.*" And he holds up a drawing for everyone to see: a picture of some big-ass capitalist pissin' all over little folk. The caption reads, *Trickle Down Economics*.

Well, Pomeroy keeps strummin' his ol' guitar, but can't sing no more verses. 'Cause that bushy-beard dude is yellin' his head off and drownin' ol' Pomeroy out. He ain't even a man of the people and he's stealin' himself my crowd. So I walk over to that supple-ass bitch who's been givin' me ol' eye. And I ask her, "What the fuck?"

The bitch, she just starts gigglin like maybe I done goosed her. "We call him Ezekiel, luvy," she says. "Some call him Zeke for short."

"Don't no one call *me* short," I say and I give her a big ol' wink. Bitch makes me think of Sweet Molly

Malone—that fish peddlin' tramp in that old Irish song. Where she's hollerin' out, *Cockles alive alive-o.*

"Zeke thinks he's a prophet," she says and her voice is all hearty and full. "He makes a bit of sense, he does, but he does drone on and on. When he's not stiffing people for drinks, that is. Or dressing up like a woman."

"How about I stiff you for nothin'?" I say.

The bitch just arches her eyebrows. "You trying to shock me, luv?" she blurts. "I'm a barmaid at the Commons Inn, you know."

Now before ol' Pomeroy can reel the bitch in, ol' Ezekiel starts blowin' a whistle. And then he starts scoldin' the New World Order.

"When the students complain about class fees," he shouts, *"does the government offer them help? NO. They blind them with pepper spray and place them under arrest.*

"When our soldiers come back from Afghanistan, do they give the poor chaps a hand? NO. They toss them in jail if they don't toe the line and leave them there to rot."

"When we catch Obama spying on us, does he issue an apology? NO. He calls Mr. Snowden a criminal and drives him into exile."

Well, the fucker keeps rollin' his eyes like they're dice and bellowin' louder 'an a fish wife. And that kinda shit gets on Pomeroy's nerves.

"They call themselves statesmen," he howls. *"They call themselves the government. But they're coming for your pensions. They're coming for your rights. They're coming for your sons to fight their bleedin'*

wars. And our real statesmen, *blokes like Edward Snowden, they drive into exile and toss into jail."*

The dude draws a deep breath, like maybe he's a blowfish. And then he starts shoutin' even louder.

"WHY HAVE THINGS COME TO THIS?!!" he booms. *"WHY HAVE THINGS COME TO THIS?!!*

"BECAUSE THAT'S WHAT DYING EMPIRES DO!!!"

Ol' Pomeroy decides to get his ass out of there. 'Cause it ain't gonna be long 'til the New World Order comes after that fucker. And snatches up Pomeroy, to boot. So I pick up my rucksack and ol' guitar and throw Molly over my shoulder. Hell, the bitch been talkin' like maybe she supports that fucker. And I don't want to see her get dragged off to jail. Not 'til I've slipped her the ol' shillelagh, I don't.

AFTER I HAUL MY ASS outta that square, I head down Patrick Street. And soon I spot me this rickety-ass pub with a sign hangin' over the door. The sign says, Bleary O'Leary's Hole. So I put ol' Molly down 'cause her yellin' is hurtin' my ears. And I invite her to join me for a nightcap. Bitch'll be needin' a stiff shot of whiskey to handle ol' Pomeroy whole.

Ol' Molly, she just looks at me and her eyes are kinda hard. Like she'd just as soon kick ol' Pomeroy's crotch as join him for a drink. But then she starts gigglin' all over again, like she's lookin' at a circus clown.

"I saw you on YouTube," she hoots. "Knockin' down cops with a guitar, you were. You're a bit of a cheeky one, aren't you, luv?"

"They call me Pomeroy," I tell the tart just to keep things straight. Can't have no piece of ass teasin' ol' Pomeroy. Not when I'm a two-star general 'an all.

Well, the bitch cocks her head like a parrot and shrugs. "Is that what they really call you?" she asks. "Or is that what you call yourself?"

The broad's got a mouth on her, that's for sure—hell, I oughta make *her* my manager. But I flex my muscles like Spartacus 'cause I gotta put her in her place. "I'm a man of the people," I tell her.

The bitch just shakes her head. "Really, luv? Is that what you are? You *do* seem more manchild than man."

Now Pomeroy, he's startin' to get pissed. If that hussy wants her potatoes plowed, she better stop talkin' smack. But Molly, she puts her hands on her hips and sticks out her melon-sized tits. And her eyes are clearer 'an emeralds.

"Luvy," she says, her voice bossy as hell. "Your mum know what you're doing?"

"Lookin' out for one of the people," I say. "An' scorin' me some ass."

Ol' Molly, she just scratches her head like she's tryin' to get rid of some lice. But she's gotta be drippin' for Pomeroy's schlong. Hell, there's no surer way to nail a bitch than to save her from the New World Order. Shit like that's gotta work every time.

"Luv," she says, "how often *do* you score? You don't have much game, do you now?"

"Ten on the slack ain't no game," I tell her. "Not when I'm gonna be a rock star, it ain't. Once I've signed me a contract with Apple, I'm gonna look after your ass."

Molly keeps on studying me and her face gets kinda soft. Like she spotted herself a puppy in a window. And all the time she's sizin' me up, I hear music comin' from the pub.

"It's a veteran's bar, luvy," she says to me softly. "You'll need to be careful in there. Lots of bars won't even serve veterans. Don't want those blokes liquored up, do they now?"

"Pomeroy's a veteran himself," I tell her. "Fought to protect our freedom."

The bitch reaches up high, straightens my collar, then takes me by the elbow. "You have too *much* freedom if you ask me, luv. Someone needs to look after *you*."

She's coverin' her mouth with her hand while she's speakin', like she's tryin' to trap herself a kiss. But her eyes are sparklin' like dew on grass and her tits are heavin' with lust. And so, with Molly Malone on my elbow, I walk into Bleary O'Leary's.

IT'S SORRY AS HELL in Bleary O'Leary's and Pomeroy feels kinda depressed. It's a dimly-lit room with an old splintered bar and a buncha dirty tables. And there's six or eight veterans at one of the tables: hairy fuckers with military hoodies and Army insignia patches. They're lookin' at this stage where some skinny-ass fucker is strummin' a ukulele. The dude's singin' a song about Blarney stones.

"*Oooooooo, why don't you kiss me Blarney stones. Come kiss me Blarney stooooones.*"

The veterans, they're laughin' and gulpin' down beer like they got nothin' better to do. Like there's no place else they'd rather be. So that's when I think me up a plan that'll keep my ass outta jail. If I entertain them dudes, like some USO fucker, the New World Order won't bother me none. 'Cause you can't be jailin' a patriot fucker who's keepin' the veterans happy. Dudes who helped snatch up the oil.

When I tell ol' Molly I got me a plan, she looks at me kinda funny. "Gonna pull a Bob Hope," I tell her. "That'll keep us out of jail for sure."

Ol' Molly, she just chuckles and chugs herself a beer. "Luvy," she giggles, "there's hope for you yet."

Well, Molly keeps on laughin', but I unpack my guitar. And I wait for that skinny fucker to stop singin' about his balls. But the dude's got more verses 'an Pomeroy does and he keeps goin' on and on. So I watch me this fuzzy-ass television that's sittin' above the bar. The local news is on and some talkin' head dude is babblin' about Afghanistan. About how Obama is pullin' out troops so to bring the war to an end. And that ticks ol' Pomeroy off for sure. If there's no troops left in Afghanistan, I won't get no chance to perform there.

When that ukulele dudes's finally done with his song, he goes to the men's room to jack off. And while he's in there floggin' his log, I hop on the stage, strum me some chords, and start singin' *The Ballad of the Green Berets*.

Put silver wings on my son's chest.
Make him one of America's Best.

I ain't sung no more 'an two fuckin' bars when one of the veterans starts talkin' smack. "*What are ya, guv?"* he shouts. *"A cheerleader for the fucking politicians?"*

"Oye," shouts another. *"He's trying to make a killing while blokes are getting killed. Just like Halliburton, he is."*

"They shoulda let us finish the mission," shouts a third who looks like he's drunk as a skunk. *"They shoulda let us finish the mission."*

"Fuck the mission!" the first one shouts. *"If ya ask me, Basil, we pointed the guns in the wrong direction!"*

Before I can sing me the tag line, them veterans have started up a chant. And their liquored-ass voices are fillin' the whole damn bar. *"Hey, hey. Ho ho. Brothers died for Amoco. HEY HEY. HO HO. BROTHERS DIED FOR AMOCO."* And then they start booin' ol' Pomeroy and bangin' their beer mugs on the table.

Well, Pomeroy strikes a coupla more chords, but those veterans keep drownin' him out. An' their beer mugs are bouncin' offa the walls and shatterin' on the floor. An' one of 'em's shakin' his fist at ol' Pomeroy an' growlin' like a bear. *"BASH THAT WANKER,"* the fucker shouts. *"HE'S A SHILL FOR THE NEW WORLD ORDER."* So Pomeroy starts singin' *Fortunate Son* to shut them fuckers up.

It ain't me. It ain't me.
I ain't no senator's son, son.
It ain't me. It ain't me...

But that don't make no never mind at all—them veterans start smashin' up tables and chairs and shoutin' up a storm. *"BLOODY HEY, BLOODY HELL! NO MORE DEATHS FOR BLOODY SHELL!"* An' a pitcher comes flyin' through the air an' explodes on the stage like a bomb.

Well, Molly Malone, she's halfway out the door already. An' she's motionin' me to follow her *quick*. Guess she can't wait no longer for a dose of my schlong—not after hearin' me singin' an' all. So I crack me a woody the size of a log and go limpin' towards the door. The woman got an ass to die for.

The bar is now louder 'an a mortar attack and the walls are startin' to shake. And a voice like creepin' thunder is fillin' the whole damn room. *"BEEEE THE CAUSE NOT GOOD..."* An' damn if ol' Ezekiel ain't standin' up on the stage. The fucker is wearin' a long gingham dress an' he's quotin' from *Henry V.*

"BEEE THE CAUSE NOT GOOD," he bellows, *"THE KINGS WILL HAVE MUCH TO ANSWER FOR COME JUDGEMENT DAY!!"*

"HO HO," the veterans shout. *"NO MORE BLOOD FOR AMOCO!!"*

"WHEN ALL THOSE ARMS AND LEGS AND HEADS BAND TOGETHER AND CRY OUT, 'WE DIED FOR THIS??!!'"

Now all that yellin' an' furniture smashin' is makin' me lose my woody. And I don't even hear the *police sirens* screamin'—not 'til some cops burst into the bar and the veterans start peltin' 'em with their medals.

One of them cops shouts, *"Oye! There's the pisser!"* I grab my guitar by the neck.

"It's him!" the cop yells. *"It's bloody Pomeroy! The Yank wot piddled on Blarney castle!"*

"Hook him up him first!" another cop shouts. *"We'll kick his arse back across the pond!"*

Well, I can't let them cops put no bracelets on me—not when I'm on Obama's list. 'Cause if I get my ass shipped to Guantánamo Bay, folks'll never see Pomeroy again. So I lift my guitar above my head and start swingin' it at their heads.

"THE ANGEL OF THE LORD HAS ARRIVED," shouts Ezekiel. *"THE ANGEL OF THE LORD IS HERE. MAY HE SMITE A THOUSAND PHILISTINES WITH HIS TERRIBLE SWEET SWORD!!!"*

Now the room keeps gettin' louder as more cops keep pourin' in. And after I've brained four or five of them fuckers, my guitar ain't nothin' but splinters. So I sing a cappella to have me an encore and damn if that don't strain my throat.

I done pissed on Blarney Castle.
I done dissed a feudal lord.
But I ain't no fuckin' vassal
And I got a ten inch sword.

A FEW OF 'EM COPS are still clingin' to me as I shove my way out the door. So I give 'em each a head butt then shake 'em loose like fleas. But now I hear a helicopter over my head an' it kinda reminds me of Nam. And Ezekiel's shoutin' *"MARTIAL LAW!!"* while the cops are draggin' him from the bar. So Pomeroy, he starts runnin' like a motherfucker.

I ain't gone more 'an two or three blocks when the Volkswagen bug stops beside me. An' ol' Molly is grippin' the steerin' wheel like maybe it's a snake. And

Molly, she looks like she's kinda upset: her blouse is disheveled, her hair is unkempt, and her face is glistenin' with sweat. But that don't stop me from crackin' a stiffy and grinnin' like a fox.

"*Hsst,*" Molly says, her voice all husky. "*Luvy. Get inside.*"

The passenger door is open wide so I manage to squeeze my ass in. But there ain't much room to pull in my legs and that kinda gets me riled. If that bitch wants to rescue me properly, she oughta be drivin' a Mercedes.

After I slam that tiny-ass door, ol' Molly guns the engine. And next thing I know, the car's squealin' 'round corners and hurtlin' down narrow streets. And Molly, she looks over at me and gives me a cut-the-crap look.

"Keep your head *down*, luvy," she hisses. "And your mouth *shut.*"

Well, there ain't much to look at anyhow—nothin' but churches and cheese shops. And them kind of sights don't snow no one but tourists. So I duck my head below the window and take me a big ol' breath. And since Molly's drivin' like a bat outta hell, I start singin', *Go, Lassie, Go.*

I will raaaaise my love a tower
By this big ol gushin' fountain
And on it I will pile
All the flooowers of the mountain...

But before I start me a second verse, ol' Molly stops the car. "No time for serenades, luvy—we're here." And when I take me a look through the window, I see me a harbor with ships.

Molly, her face is mellow now and her eyes are softer 'an shit. "This is Cork Harbor, luv," she tells me. "Immigrants left for the new world from here. During the potato famine, that was."

"They shoulda ate your cockles," I tell her.

Ol' Molly points towards the dock. "Wait on the jetty. Me brother has a fishing boat. He'll be picking you up and taking you to Bristol."

Well, the water is blacker 'an ink and the whitecaps are whisperin' like ghosts. So Pomeroy ain't in no hurry to get in no shaky-ass boat. But Molly, she looks like a dame in distress so I puff out my chest like ol' Sinbad.

But Molly ain't lookin' at Pomeroy no more—she's starin' out onto the bay. The look in her eyes—like she's listenin' to distant music—reminds me of that spinner wife in Joyce's *The Dead*.

"Me son had a fine Irish voice," she says softly. "Until he came back from Iraq. The smoke mucked his lungs up, didn't it now?"

Ol' Molly starts hummin' *Danny Boy* an' then she pats my cheek. "Bristol's in Wales in case you don't know it. You can't get there on the ferry, you know. The coppers will nab you if you try."

"Ain't nobody takin' down Pomeroy." I say. "Pomeroy's built to last."

"You'll last a lot longer in Scotland, luv. Hitch a ride to the Highlands, if you can. It's hard to arrest a bloke if he's hiding in the hills of Scotland."

Before Pomeroy can explore ol' *Molly's* hills, the bitch starts singin' *The Green Fields of France*. A song about graveyards and playin' a fife and bangin' a drum too slow. The bitch oughta be bangin' ol' Pomeroy—not singin' some spooky-ass song.

"Already got me a caber," I say. "And I don't want it splittin' my pants."

Ol Molly, she starts laughin' out loud and she gives me a poke on the chest. "Luvy, I'm not going to shag you, you know. You'll have to take care of it yourself. I imagine you're rather good at it by now."

I guess the bitch is abstaining from meat if she don't want a taste of my schlong. But Pomeroy likes 'em brassy so I'm still gonna hire her butt.

"Gonna let you schedule my groupies," I tell her. "Gonna let you be my manager."

"Really, luv? Is that what you're going to do?"

"Gonna make you so rich you won't have to sell cockles no more. And your son'll be proud of your ass."

Ol' Molly, she just shakes her head and then she starts hummin' again. "Luvy," she says to me finally, "he died in Wandsworth Prison."

IT SURE DIDN'T HURT ol' Pomeroy none to kiss that Blarney Stone. 'Cause after I watch ol' Molly drive off, I hear some new verses to *Ants in My Pants*. So I sit my ass on the dock of the bay and sing 'em out loud an' clear.

The New World Order's got us covered
They say our future will be bright
If we give 'em all our money
And we give 'em all our rights

If we let 'em grab the planet
If we let 'em sell their wars
But they ain't a jivin' Pomeroy
'Cause my pecker's twice as large.

Ol' Pomeroy, he's singin' without no guitar, but I'm still gettin' lotsa support. I can hear me the blarin' of freighters. I can hear me the clangin' of buoys. I can hear the shrieks of seagulls all pleadin' like groupies in heat. And I can hear the drum-drum-drummin' of the police helicopters overhead.

Guess the New World Order's still huntin' my ass, but that don't amount to shit. They ain't catchin Pomeroy—that's for sure. I'll be hidin' somewhere in the Highlands.

4.
Pomeroy &
The Last Supper

AFTER MOLLY SAVED ME from them Irish cops, I lit out for Bristol with her brother in a tiny-ass fishin' boat. And the bitch was in such a hurry to see me cast off that she left me with a big ol' stiffy. So Pomeroy was limpin' like Long John Silver after hoppin' aboard that boat. But my whanger shrunk *quick* when we hit the bounding main. 'Cause them whitecaps were snarlin' like wolves on the hunt and soakin' ol' Pomeroy to the bone. Molly shoulda given me a cup of bouillon before puttin' me on that boat. Maybe then I'd 'a' kept my woody.

Well, after we crossed that howlin' sea, we tied up in Bristol Harbor. And Molly Malone's brother, who looks like Captain Nemo, gave me a fifty pound bill. He told me to buy me some fish an' chips. He told me to buy a warm hat. And he told me to keep dodgin' Obama's goons. 'Cause his nephew done fought for Obama in Iraq then couldn't get no medical care for his lungs. He said Obama can stick that Arab oil up his ass and Prime Minister Cameron can get himself fucked. He said to keep singin' my subversive-ass songs 'cause the world needs to hear that shit. So I sang some new verses to *Ants in My Pants* as I strolled towards the city of Bristol.

> *I done bashed some Irish coppers*
> *Then I crossed the Celtic Sea*
> *'Cause I piddle where I wanna*
> *And a warrant's out on me.*

> *So I'll hide out in the Highlands*
> *While they're makin' me a star*
> *And I'll sing,* This land is my land
> *When I get me a guitar.*

BEFORE TOO LONG, I'm walkin' down King Street, this historic-ass street fulla churches and pubs and fish shops that smell like pussy. And I come to this pub called Llandoger Trow where *Treasure Island* was wrote. I read *Treasure Island* a dozen times when I was workin' in the library at Quentin. 'Cause Long John Silver got it right. Don't be mannin' no ship for some greedy-ass squire who ain't gonna share no gold with you. Not when you can grab a big pot of it for yourself and start up a chain of seafood restaurants.

Well, I spot me some cops on King Street so I get my butt outta there quick. 'Cause *Ants in My Pants* is on the Internet now. And if some groupies start squealin' for my schlong, the cops are gonna swarm all over me. And throw my ass in Guantánamo Bay for dissin' the New World Order. Hell, a fucker can't do *concerts* if he's stuck in Guantánamo Bay. The place is fulla Arabs who don't listen' to nothin' but lutes.

When I find me this pawnshop on Baldwin Street, I duck my ass inside. And I buy me a second hand Gibson guitar. It's got a good long neck for fingerin' chords and a good strong body for bashin' cops. And it only cost me thirty-five Lizzies.

Well, I don't see no cops when I leave the pawnshop so I whistle me a tune. Just like the Happy Wanderer done—that yodeling-ass fucker who sings, *Valderi valdera.* Then I sing some new verses to *Ant in My Pants.*

Well, I'm headin' for the Highlands
Where the babes are hot to trot
'Cause Obama hates my lyrics
And that fucker don't forget.

But I'll vanish like Houdini
If the cops start closin' in
And I'll stroke my big ol' weenie
While I'm hidin' in a glen.

WELL, AFTER I BUY ME SOME FISH and chips, I sit my ass in Castle Park. And when I'm done eatin', I call Pocahontas on the cell phone she let me have. And I tell her I'm gonna hide out in the Highlands while Apple is makin' me famous.

Pocahontas, she tells me that ain't gonna work. She says my face is all over the news and Cameron wants me jailed *bad.* 'Cause he don't like fuckers who piddle on shrines and piss off the New World Order.

She says half the police in the British Isles are lookin' for me now. And I'm gonna end up in Guantánamo Bay if I don't leave the UK quick.

Pocahontas, she tells me I'd best head for France. 'Cause the French ain't *fightin'* in no oil grabbin' wars. And the French ain't *eatin'* no freedom fries. She says if I get myself over to France, ain't no one gonna extradite my ass.

Well, Pomeroy he don't parlez-vous no français. But I seen *An American in Paris*—that tap dancin' movie with Gene Kelly in it. So I know all about them sidewalk cafés and how to get mademoiselles damp for your shank. Hell, the language in France is the language of *love*. And don't *nobody* speak that better 'an Pomeroy.

I STILL GOT A BUNCHA LIZZIES in my pocket so I buy me a megabus ticket to Paris. I also buy a beret in a thrift shop since I need me a disguise. And I pull that beret down over my eyes as I haul my ass onto that bus. 'Cause if I look like I'm a Frenchman, the cops won't bother me none.

After I find me my seat on the bus, I notice a coupla dry puss bitches starin' at me. Like maybe they don't believe I'm no Frenchman. So I put my guitar on my lap and start strummin' it. And then I start singin' a song about France—the only song I know. I remember it from *Gigi*, this classic-ass flick with Maurice Chevalier that I watched in the library in Quentin. So I sing me a coupla bars from *Gigi*.

Each time I see a leetle girl

Of five or seex or seven,
I can't reseest a joyous yell an' then I cry,
Thank Heaven. Thank Heaven for leetle girls...

Them dowager bitches start glarin' at Pomeroy and then they change their seats. But don't nobody bother me none after that—not even when the bus is speedin' through England, not even when the French border guards check my passport, not even when the bus eases onto this train and we shoot through the Channel Tunnel. Ten hours later, still wearin' my beret, I'm standin' in the City of Love. And I done changed my Lizzies to euros.

Well, I'm standin' by the Seine, watchin' some kids cast for minnows, when I give Pocahontas another call on my cell phone. When I tell her I'm in Paris, she says I'm lucky as shit. She says Cameron done called me a terrorist for beatin' up them cops. And my mug shot's been posted in half the newspapers in the United Kingdom. And the only reason I made it to Paris is that someone weren't payin' attention.

She also says Charlemagne's still in jail and they're chargin' him with conspiring to import terrorism. And the New World Order done posted his mug shot on the Internet. 'Cause the New World Order wants to smear him too and keep his ass in jail.

Well, it looks like ol' Pomeroy better lay low and not piss off no Frogs. So I pull my beret back down over my eyes and I take me a leisurely stroll.

OL' POMEROY AIN'T ever seen nothin' like Paris. There's fountains and statues around every corner.

There's cafés on every block with artists sellin' cheap-ass paintings. There's pickpockets all over the place, scoutin' out the tourists. And the air is fulla 'lectricity everywhere I walk.

But I *shouda* come to Paris in the twenties when the Lost Generation was here. I'd have balled ol' Alice B. Toklas. I'd have sipped tea with Gertrude Stein. And when ol' James Joyce heard *Ants in My Pants*, he'd have made me the toast of the town. It wouldn't have taken so long to get famous if I'd 'a' come here in the twenties.

But I'm still gonna soak me up some culture. So after I spend a night on a park bench, I catch a Métro bus to the Louvre. It's only 8:00 a.m. when I get there, but there's already a mile-long line of tourists waitin' to get in. So Pomeroy, he stands in line with them fuckers and waits for two whole hours. And I hum me some show tunes from *Gigi* so folks will think I'm a Frenchman.

When I finally get into the South Lobby of the Louvre, I ain't exactly blown away. There's big-dicked paintings all over the walls, but folks ain't stoppin' to look at 'em. Instead, they're scurryin' like mice through the halls to see the *Mona Lisa*. Like the rest of the paintings don't mean crap. No wonder it's hard for a dude to sell his music. Unless you're already famous, people ain't gonna look at you twice.

Well, I follow the crowd to this jam-packed room where the *Mona Lisa* is hung. And someone done cut a fart in there so the room smells kinda like a john. And Mona Lisa, she's studyin' the tourists from behind this bullet-proof glass. Her expression is kinda disgusted—like she ain't got no use for them lemming-ass fuckers.

But she's also sizin' up Pomeroy like she's wantin' a spin on my schlong. 'Cause that would put a *real* smile on her face.

Well Pomeroy, he don't like pushin' through crowds just to be *lookin'* at a piece of ass. So I check me out the rest of the Louvre. I see me Napoleon's apartments. I see me some crazy-ass ceilings. And I see me ol' Venus, the goddess of love—this armless chick what can't give no hand jobs.

After a while, I check out the Grand Gallery. That's where *The Da Vinci Code* was filmed—that lame-ass flick with *The Last Supper* in it. But I don't see no crazy-eyed monks killin' folks 'cause the Church lost touch with its feminine side. I just see tourists chasin' their kids 'stead of lookin' at Renaissance art.

I read me *The Da Vinci Code* only once 'cause *The Last Supper* ain't that mysterious. There ain't no yin and yang in it. There ain't no pussy in it. And that dude next to Jesus what looks like a woman is just some fucker without a beard. Don't guess ol' Jesus had much use for women. The dude couldn't get a rise 'til the third day.

Well ol' Pomeroy, he starts gettin' tired of the Louvre. There's too many dumb fucks in it. There's too many screamin' kids. And the air conditioning don't work for shit. So I find me this staircase exit and I make my way out to the street. Then I take me a walk in the Paris sunshine.

I SPEND THE AFTERNOON ridin' buses and takin' in the sights. I see me the Pantheon. I see me the Arc de Triomphe. I see the Eiffel Tower, which reminds me of Pomeroy's dong. Don't none of these sights impress me too much 'cause I already seen 'em in the movies. But when I visit me Pompidou Center, I see something I ain't *never* seen before. I see a dozen bitches, all of 'em butt naked, carryin' signs and shoutin' at the top of their lungs. They got big black letters painted on their bodies—letters that spell *Fuck Putin, Fuck The Church*, and *Fuck Your Morals*. And a few of 'em are squattin' over eight-by-ten photos of some imperial lookin' fucker. And they're pissin' all over the fucker's face. If this is the yin to the Church's yang, *The Da Vinci Code* got it wrong.

Well, Pomeroy ain't passin' up buck naked bitches even if they *are* ravin' mad. So I trot over to where they're demonstratin' and strum the ol' guitar. Then I snatch me one of their pamphlets to see if they maybe like Dylan. The pamphlet says, *WE ARE FEMEN. BARE BREASTS ARE OUR WEAPONS. WE FIGHT PATRIARCHY IN ALL ITS FORMS.* Don't know if bare breasts are weapons or not, but Pomeroy ain't complainin'.

Now them butt naked bitches are drawin' a crowd and I see a handful of cops standin' by. So I decide to keep actin' like a Frenchman—just to play it safe. So I sing 'em *Frère Jacques* 'cause I know the French words to that. I saw it performed on *Sesame Street* once.

Frère Jacques! Frère Jacques!
Dormez-vous? Dormez-vous?
Sonnez les matines, sonnez les matines.
Ding-dang-dong, ding-dang-dong.

Well, a few of them bitches start givin' Pomeroy the ol' eye. 'Cause there's nothin' like a French lullaby to get a pussy slick. And I hear 'em talkin' French to each other.

"Qu'est-ce que c'est que ce *ding-dong*?"

"On dirait un malheureux sans-abri."

"*Non, non. C'est Monsieur Pomeroy.* Il tabasse les flics."

"*Monsieur Pomeroy?!* Je l'ai entendu chanter sur *YouTube.* C'est le roi des cochons."

"If Monsieur Pomeroy beats up police," one of 'em says in English, "he can't be a *complete* pig, oui? Even if he sings piggish songs."

The bitches keep jabberin' for a while then one of 'em walks over to me. She's a tall blonde spinner with heavy tits and a snatch that looks like a mango. And she's lookin' at me with this half-baked smile, just like Mona Lisa done.

"Monsieur Pom'roy," she purrs in this kittenish voice. "Would you help us do a skit? A little street theater, s'il vous plaît."

Well, I thrust out my hips like Elvis so she'll know I can fuck me a harem. And I give her a big ol' Jack Nicholson grin so she'll know I got actor's blood. If ya wanna impress European chicks, ya gotta be suave as shit.

"Oui Oui," I say and I look at her muff.

The bitch, she just chuckles and rolls her eyes. "He *sounds* like a pig, does he not?" she says. The rest of 'em start to laugh.

Well next thing I know, I'm sittin' on the ground and them bitches are tyin' me up. They're bindin' my ankles and wrists with their bras and gigglin' just like schoolgirls. And when they're done tyin' ol' Pomeroy up, the blonde one sticks an apple in my mouth. Then she blows me a kiss, bows to the crowd, and performs a pirouette. And some women in the crowd start applaudin' like crazy and laughin' their tits off.

But Pomeroy, he's startin' to get kinda miffed. Hell, I can't have no spinner treatin' me like a pig—that ain't good for my image. And my mood don't get no better when the bitch sketches a charcoal portrait of me. 'Cause after she's done drawin' that picture, she puts it on the ground. And the rest of 'em take turns squattin' over it and peein' on Pomeroy's likeness.

Well, them tarts are still squatin' and peein' when the cops come closin' in. And the cops start grabbin' 'em left and right and forcin' 'em to the ground. And the bitches keep linkin' their arms together so the cops can't haul 'em off. And a few of 'em are pumpin' fists in the air and shoutin' out slogans in French. But it ain't too long 'til they're all rounded up and sittin' in a circle. And then they start singin' some French-ass anthem, which gotta be 'bout revolution. And the cops, they're all just standin' around like they ain't sure what to do next.

Well, *Pomeroy* knows what to do next—even if he's all tied up. So after I rip myself free of them bras, I waltz on over to them cops. And I head butt three or four of 'em and leave 'em dazed on the ground. 'Cause them Frenchy cops ain't got no business stealing ol' Pomeroy's harem. Then I snatch up that blonde chick, the one with the mango pussy, and throw her over my shoulder. And I grab my guitar while she's kickin' and screamin'. Gonna need it to get her all juiced for my spruce.

I'm startin' to feel some déjà vu as I carry that bitch away. 'Cause grabbin' up pussy and cartin' it off is becoming a bit of a habit. But when a woman struts around bare-ass naked—and ties up Pomeroy to boot— she don't *deserve* no slack.

I HEAD BUTT ME the rest of them cops before leaving Pompidou Center. Hadda get 'em outta my way. And that's hard to do with a bitch on your back and a big ol' guitar in your hand. But I gotta hang onto my ol' guitar so's to keep the pussies drippin'. Can't be breakin' it over the heads of no cops.

After I knock out the last of them fuckers, my head is about to explode. But I take off lickity split with the bitch hangin' over my shoulder. 'Cause if Pomeroy don't move like a motherfucker, he's gonna be back in jail.

Well, I ain't gone more 'an a block or two before I drop the bitch on the sidewalk. 'Cause it's hard to be carryin' a swoonin' broad when my shoulders are achin' like shit. If a woman wants a fucker to whisk her away, like he's Rudolph Valentino in *The Sheik*, she'd better be keepin' her weight down.

The bitch, she don't bother apologizin' for gettin' my shoulders all cramped up. She just looks at me with these smoky eyes that remind me of Venus de Milo. But she's holdin' up a pair of *hands* 'cause her wrists are flex-cuffed together. Guess she can't be freein' ol' Pomeroy's schlong if she don't have full use of her hands.

"Monsieur Pom'roy," she gasps. "My wrists, s'il vous plaît."

115

Her breath cools my neck as I pull loose them flex cuffs. And her voice is all shaky as she starts to rub her wrists. "May I have the loan of your shirt, Monsieur Pom'roy?"

Now Pomeroy, he's a gentleman so I hand her over my shirt. And she grabs it from me and slips it on quick. 'Cause she don't want no one but Pomeroy to be gettin' a view of her snatch. But when I flex my muscles like Rudolph Valentino, I feel my crotch explode. Like someone done tossed a grenade under me. Damn if that bitch didn't kick me in the balls.

Well, I'm sittin' flat on my ass, massagin' my busted nuts, when the broad kinda changes her tune. "Pom'roy," she purrs. "You deserved that, Monsieur. Now you must come with me, please."

What's *deserved* is a butt kickin'—that's for sure—and the bitch is the one who deserves it. But Pomeroy ain't gonna slap her around 'cause it looks like she's psyched for my spike. And Pomeroy don't screw pussy that's black-and-blue. So after I get myself back to my feet, I follow her to this subway station. And I sing some new verses to *Ants in My Pants* as I follow her down the escalator

I done rescued me a damsel
Who done kicked me in the nuts.
Now I'm gonna limp and stumble
While I'm followin' her butt.

But when she rips apart my zipper,
She'll be in for a surprise
'Cause my balls won't be too chipper
And my dick ain't gonna rise.

Well, it ain't but a second or two 'til this train comes rollin' to a stop. And that blonde chick, she pushes me onto the train before I can make up more verses. But the train is packed with people, which pisses ol' Pomeroy off. 'Cause I need to be parkin' my ass on a seat and restin' my throbbin' nuts.

TEN MINUTES LATER, when we hop off the train, my nuts ain't feelin' no better. So I limp like I got frog legs and follow the bitch to the street. And the broad is in such a hurry, she don't even slow down her pace. She don't even stop at no sidewalk café to order me some snails. Gonna need me a few of them escargots to wake my pecker up.

When we come to this dingy-looking part of town, my bladder is startin' to burst. So I find me a tree and take me a leak. And I hum *C'est Si Bon* so folks will still think I'm a Frenchman. And the bitch, she's watchin' me shake my dick like she'd like to be wieldin' a sword. With her sharp-ass cheekbones and hungry eyes, she looks kinda like a Viking queen.

"Monsieur," she says. "You should be in a cage. Why is it you are not?!"

Well, I stuff my pecker back into my pants so she won't be bitin' it off. And I give her a sly ol' wink. "Got me a guardian angel," I say.

"Only *one* angel," she laughs. "You need a whole flock of them, perhaps."

"What I need is a manager," I say. "A chick to book my concerts 'stead of runnin' around butt naked."

The bitch just gives me this savvy-ass look. "A woman to order around, don't you mean? A woman you can fuck like a whore."

"If you want a Pomeroy fuckin'," I say, "you better be managing me right. You gotta *earn* a Pomeroy hump."

The chick, she bursts out laughin' and then she starts shakin' her head. "What a *pig* you are," she says. "But what a funny pig." And she keeps on laughin' and wipin' her eyes like she's lookin' at Charlie Chaplin.

When the bitch is done laughin', her face gets all pious like maybe she's Joan of Arc. "Pom'roy," she says. "Come with me, please. I must return your shirt."

WELL, I FOLLOW THE BITCH down some narrow streets, all the time limpin' like Long John, and we come to the place where them women live. It's this giant-ass room what looks like a factory warehouse. And there ain't nothin' in it but some ratty furniture, a dozen cots, and this big ol' punchin' bag hangin' from the ceiling. The bitch must use that punchin' bag to practice kickin' fuckers in the nuts. 'Cause she's pretty goddamn good at it.

After the bitch puts a minidress on, and gives me back my shirt, we have ourselves a chat. Turns out she's from the Ukraine and her name is Oxsana Chaplinsky. Turns out she been given asylum in France along with her sister sextremists. 'Cause the cops in Kiev, what don't like bare-titted demonstrators, done hid a grenade where them hussies was livin'. And a picture of Putin with a bullseye on his face. The cops done set them bitches up to look like jive-ass terrorists.

So the bunch of 'em hauled their asses to Paris so they wouldn't get put in no communist jail. And now they're livin' in Paris and expandin' their organization. 'Cause most of them bitches are fluent in French and wanna become French citizens.

Well, I don't know why she's tellin' me this—ol' Pomeroy don't give a shit. 'Cept that I need me a manager to book my concerts for me. And maybe some groupies to pass out my albums and bleed ol' Pomeroy's seed. 'Cause my *whanger*, that's what's expandin' right now. So I pick up my Gibson guitar and sing some brand new verses.

Well, I'm hidin' out with Femen
With more coppers on my ass
'Cause them chicks are starved for semen
And my balls are made of brass.

So I'll make 'em all my harem
And I'll fuck 'em from behind
Hope my big ol' schlong don't scare 'em
'Cause it's time for me to shine.

While Pomeroy's strummin' his ol' guitar, the rest of them floozies, now wearin' jeans and Femen sweatshirts, come driftin' into the room. Guess the coppers couldn't detain 'em too long since they got political asylum. But when the bitches see Pomeroy singin' away, they start talkin' 'bout *his* asylum. Like maybe they don't want no chauvinist pig hidin' out where they live and train. But Oxsana, she starts lecturin' 'em in her clipped-ass English. She tells 'em the cops I brained done needed a head bashin'. She

119

says I been treatin' her like a lady. She says if their movement is gonna succeed, they gotta show more tolerance than the pigs. And poor ol' Pomeroy, he's on the run after defendin' Femen's honor.

Well, them hussies they have a discussion and decide to give Pomeroy asylum. But that don't settle things for long. Soon some faggoty dude what looks like a hustler comes slinkin' into the room. A swishy-ass fucker with a pencil-thin moustache and a fedora on his head. And the dude starts cussin' the bitches in French like he ain't too happy with 'em. And then he starts kickin' 'em left and right with these stiletto-toed boots. And the broads, they don't be arguin' with that fucker—they just try an' stay outta his way.

Now when that dipshit notices Pomeroy, he starts to act even worse. His eyes start bulgin' out like grapes and he starts cussin' up a storm. Don't know what he's sayin', but it's clear he don't want me around. And it's clear he's gonna punish them broads for harborin' 'emselves a stud.

Well, it looks like these feminists have got 'emselves a pimp daddy. A fucker who's taken advantage of 'em 'cause they're simple Ukrainian girls. And who's probably makin' a bundle by sellin' Femen t-shirts. But I ask Oxsana anyhow just who that asshole is. Oxsana, she just cringes and then she shakes her head. She tells me his name is Pierre and he's put himself in charge. She says he controls all their money and is all the time gettin' upset. She tells me I better beware of Pierre.

Well, it don't take Pomeroy very long to handle ol' Pierre. That's Pomeroy's harem he's kickin' around and I don't like my pussy bruised. So I march on over to ol' Pierre and head-butt him right in the nose. And the fucker, he goes sprawlin' onto the floor with his nostrils gushin' blood.

After Pierre crawls out of the building, bleedin' like a pig that's been stuck, ol' Pomeroy does a beefcake pose. So's to let them cows know that they got a new bull—a stud what don't pitch for the pink team. But although my biceps are bulgin' like coconuts, them bitches look kinda confused. So Oxsana, she seizes herself the moment. Hoppin' onto a table, she shouts "*Fuck Pierre*," and pumps her fist high in the air.

"*Salut*," she cries. "*Salut Monsieur Pom'roy. Vive la liberté.*"

Them broads, they all start beamin' and Pomeroy can't blame 'em for that. Hell, they couldn't be gettin' no beamin' at all from that faggoty-ass Pierre. So I shout "*Liberté*" along with Oxsana and give 'em a crocodile grin. Then I try to decide me which ones to fuck first.

I SPEND ME A WEEK in the Femen camp, sleepin' on a couch and hidin' from the cops. And don't none of them broads jump ol' Pomeroy's stump. Guess they're all practicin' the rites of Sappho and dunno what a real man can do. But Pomeroy, he just takes his time and waits for them babes to thaw out. 'Cause there ain't no lesbo alive ol' Pomeroy can't turn straight. So I stroke my ol' Johnson through my pants and I watch them bitches train. I watch 'em do squat thrusts. I watch 'em do pushups. I watch 'em do tacklin' drills. I even watch 'em whip out their tits while they're dressed up in nun costumes.

Well, the food in that Femen camp ain't shit 'cause none of them broads can cook. So I finally decide to find me a café and have me some vichyssoise and crepes. But Oxsana, she tells me I gotta lay low and not be walkin' the streets. 'Cause the cops got a price on Pomeroy's head. And *Libération*, Paris' main newspaper, ran an article on me last week. Oxsana shows me the article, but Pomeroy don't read French. So she translates it for me in her clipped-ass English voice.

"On Tuesday," she reads me, "the peace of Pompidou Center was broken so very rudely. The saboteur, a Yankee some call Pom'roy, interrupted a demonstration by the demoiselles of Femen. After putting on a shocking display of bondage, Monsieur Pom'roy would not leave when confronted by the constabulary. Instead, he punched six policemen with a blackjack, giving each of them a concussion. Afterwards, he seized one of the demoiselles and carried her off on his back. It is doubtless Monsieur Pom'roy had rape in mind."

Oxsana, she stops readin' and looks at me real close. "Monsieur," she says, "I should be very much afraid of you."

Well, Pomeroy he's startin' to get kinda pissed. Hell, the New World Order done wrote that shit and it wants to give rape a bad name. "Let's have us a butt fuck for freedom," I say and I give her a Pomeroy wink.

Oxsana, she just kinda frowns and then she keeps on readin'. "Monsieur Pom'roy, who is on the run from the CIA and Government Communication Headquarters, is believed to be a Jihadist. He is also a flasher, a sexual predator, and a singer of pornographic songs. Those with information regarding this person are advised to contact the constabulary immediately. A handsome reward is offered for information leading to the capture of Monsieur Pom'roy."

Oxsana puts down the article and her face gets kinda tight. Then she picks up my hand and inspects my palm, like she wants to make sure I ain't jacked myself off. "Monsieur," she says, "your fortune looks so sad. I think you will soon be in jail."

"Gonna make *me* a fortune," I tell the bitch. "Gonna sign me a contract with Apple."

"Like the apple I put in your mouth?" she jokes and she squeezes the palm of my hand.

"Gonna be a rock star," I tell the bitch. "They can't put no *rich* dude in jail"

"Who said you will be a rock star?" she says.

"A fucker named Charlemagne."

"Charlemagne," she laughs. "Mon Dieu, Monsieur Pom'roy. I saw on my Facebook that *he* is in jail."

Well, I guess Oxsana been spendin' some time on the Internet. And someone done sent her ol' Charlemagne's mug shot—some fucker who thinks he's a hero for throwin' chicken blood on cops. But Oxsana, she kinda reads my mind and then she shakes her head. "He's our *groupie*, Monsieur Pom'roy—did you not know?! He comes to all our demonstrations—him and his friends with devil masks. He calls me his warrior queen."

Oxsana starts to chuckle and her smile kinda reaches her eyes. "One day, I was singing *Je T'aime Moi Non Plus*, a beautiful love song the Church calls pornographic. Monsieur Charlemagne said I sing like

Marlene Dietrich and offered a record contract to me. He said millions would hear my fabulous voice. He said Femen's cause would sweep the whole world."

Oxsana, she starts laughin' and then she strokes my head. "I never received a contract, Monsieur. What a stooge you are to trust someone who calls himself Charlemagne."

Oxsana tells me it ain't no surprise that Charlemagne's been hustlin' her ass. 'Cause stupid-ass men done hustled the Church and stupid-ass men done sold us their wars and Charlemagne, he ain't nothin' but another stupid-ass man.

After the bitch is done lecturin' my butt, she picks up my guitar. And she sits herself on a table and strums her a coupla chords. And then she starts singin' *License to Kill*—this song Dylan wrote before he done a big-ass Chrysler commercial. And her voice is deep and hollow like it's comin' from her gut.

Man is opposed to fair play.
He wants it all and he wants it his way.
But there's a woman on my block.
She just sits there as the night grows stiiiill.
She says, Whoooo's going to take away his license to kill?

When the bitch is done singin', she puts my guitar down and has herself a cry. And then she gives me this gentle-ass peck on the cheek. You can't never tell what a woman's gonna do—they're all of 'em bat shit crazy.

"Monsieur Pom'roy," she murmurs. "Je t'aime."

AFTER I BEEN in that camp for a week, a funny thing starts to happen. Whenever them broads turn a radio on—and they listen to *lots* of radio—I don't hear nothin' but *Ants in My Pants*. It's on all the rock stations. It's on all the classical music stations. It's even on them government stations what don't air nothin' but wheat reports. And them radio announcers keep blabbin' away, talkin' in both English and French. They're sayin' how *Ants in My Pants* is a great proletarian song. They're sayin' the genius what wrote that song needs to come forward and meet his public. They sayin' my music will soon sweep the world and that ain't no jive-ass shit. So it don't come as no surprise when Charlemagne calls my cell phone.

Charlemagne tells me he's out of jail now 'cause his daddy bailed him out. And that *Ants in My Pants* is airin' all over Europe—'cept for the dirty lyrics. He says I gotta sign my contract quick 'cause the royalties will be pourin' in. And I gotta grant foreign rights too so it can be translated into Italian, Russian, and German. Charlemagne says to meet him under the Eiffel Tower. 'Cause there's always a big-ass crowd there and the cops ain't gonna spot me. He says to meet him there at noon.

Well, Pomeroy ain't too happy that it's taken this long to get famous. And that he's gotta haul his ass to the Eiffel Tower just to sign some papers. Hell, Charlemagne oughta be fetchin' me there in a goddamn limousine. But I need to get outta this building for awhile 'cause my clothes smell kinda like smoke. Them commie bitches are always smokin' and that ain't good for my health. So I tell Oxsana I got me an errand to do. I tell her ol' Charlemagne done come through and I gotta go hustle my music. And as soon as I'm famous as Elvis, which won't take more 'an a day, I'll come back and fuck 'em all.

Oxsana don't seem to hear me—she's starin' out an open window. A crowd is collectin' across the street and it's chantin' anti-Femen slogans. And some granny-ass bitches are shoutin' *"Allez-vous-en"* and holdin' up pictures of Jesus.

"Monsieur Pom'roy," Oxsana says after awhile. "I think you will soon be in jail."

"They can't put no rock star in jail," I tell her. "My groupies will break the gates down. Like them fuckers what stormed the Bastille."

The crowd is chantin' louder now and Oxsana closes the window. And she looks at me with watery eyes. "Monsieur," she says. "Are revolutions not betrayed?"

The bitch got something in her hand what looks like a Saint Christopher medal. That's a coin they done made for some beefy saint who liked to carry folks across rivers. A dude what got himself famous just for haulin' folks around like a horse.

Oxsana, she sighs and blushes like she's ready to take confession. "We despise the *Church*, Monsieur Pom'roy," she says. "Saint Christopher is another matter. He's the patron saint of travelers, did you know?"

Oxsana puts the medal in my palm and folds my fingers over it. And she brushes my big-ass knuckles with her lips then pats me on the wrist. The bitch got this squirrely look on her face and she's starin' back out the window. "I think things are coming to a head, Monsieur."

Well, I crack me a woody what's hard as a raft, but I'm gonna have to leave her drippin'. 'Cause the crowd across the street is gettin' restless and it won't be long 'til the cops come snoopin' around. So I grab me up my ol' guitar and haul ass out the door.

Don't nobody try and get in my face as I push my way through the crowd. 'Cause I got my beret down over my eyes and I got a shit-eatin' grin on my face. And I keep on sayin' "S'il vous plaît" to remind folks I'm a Frenchman.

Now once ol' Pomeroy's clear of the crowd, I go lookin' for a Métro bus. A clock on a church says it's almost noon and I got me a date with destiny. So I strum my guitar while I'm walkin' along like the Happy Wanderer done. And I sing, "Valderi, valdera."

A HALF HOUR LATER, I hop off the Métro and walk towards the Eiffel Tower. It's a skyscrapin' building what's made of wrought iron and stands straighter 'an Pomeroy's schlong. And there's fountains gushin' everywhere and pigeons pickin' up crumbs.

Well, the place is packed with tourists and I don't see Charlemagne nowhere. So I have me a seat in the Jules Verne Café and order me a chili dog. Now that I'm gonna be bigger 'an Elvis the King, I gotta get used to fine restaurants.

Before the waiter can bring me my hotdog, I see Charlemagne standin' outside. It ain't no problem spottin' that dude—he's skinnier 'an a beanpole and taller 'an an ostrich. And his chin is so weak he got no chin at all. So I leave the waiter a cheap-ass tip 'cause the fucker was actin' huffy. And I haul my butt back to the street.

As soon as Charlemagne spots me, he lets out an Indian whoop. "Mighty Crockett," he bellows. "The people are saved. The earth will gush honey and milk." And he runs on over to me and throws his arms 'round my neck. And gives me this faggoty kiss on the mouth.

After that fucker done smooched me, he hands me a paper and pen. "Sign for proletariat," he shouts. "Sign for the chattel Obama has conned into fighting an oil mogul's war. Sign for the fall of anthems and corporate marionettes. May the masses awake to a nobler ballad, O Mighty, Mighty Crockett."

I'm barely done signin' the contract when I see French cops closin' in. There's fifty or sixty of 'em, all wearin' helmets and body armor, and they're comin' from every direction. And they're movin' stiff as puppets, which I guess they kinda are.

Well, I yank my guitar off my shoulder *quick* and start swingin' it right and left. And I hear ol' Charlemagne shout, "*Huzzah*" as I start knockin' cops off their feet. But I ain't sure who he's cheerin' for 'cause the fucker done set me up.

When I've knocked down half a dozen cops, my guitar ain't nothin' but pulp. So I break me off the neck and start bashin' 'em with that. And when the neck snaps in two, I start kickin' the fuckers in the nuts. But that don't do no good—they're wearin' athletic cups.

Well, Pomeroy's arms are gettin' tired so I don't feel nothin' like Crockett. I feel like ol' Beowulf musta felt when that treasure-guardin' dragon—the last one he done fought—kicked his sword-swingin' ass. 'Cause no matter how many cops I knock down, they keep comin' at me like wolves. And after they drag my ass to the ground, I'm too winded to shake 'em off. But I got enough wind for a coupla more verses and I sing 'em like the King.

Charlemagne done set my butt up
So's to beat himself a charge
'Cause Obama got my number
And he don't want me at large.

But I got me back my woody
And I ain't no kinda bitch
For them New World Order moguls
That Obama's makin' rich.

AFTER THEM COPS triple-cuff me, and toss me into a paddy wagon, they take me to this jail called Fleury-Mérogis—the biggest jail ol' Pomeroy's ever seen. It's four stories high, pentagon-shaped, and its walls are grayer 'an battleships. And there's steel cables crisscrossin' the building tops to prevent helicopter escapes. And outside the main gate, there's uniformed prison guards holdin' up picket signs and shoutin' stuff in French. They gotta be protestin' their workin' condition 'cause the place don't look too welcomin'.

Some guards what ain't out demonstratin' come and hustle my ass through a courtyard. And I can see why them picketers are upset. There's inmates yellin' from the cell blocks everywhere—hollerin' through narrow windows—and they're dumpin' their trash on the ground outside. Seems like the cons got the run of the place 'cause there ain't enough guards to handle 'em all. And some of them fuckers look dangerous as shit.

Well, the guards march me along to this intake unit what smells like cabbages and feet. And after they shine a flashlight up my ass and dress me in prison blues, they escort me to this rowdy range that's crammed fulla Arab fuckers. And them dudes are singin' Arab songs that sound kinda like cats gettin' fucked.

Once ol' Pomeroy's been shoved into a cell, this female guard starts chattin' me up in English. A scrawny little bitch with restless eyes who's wet for my ten inch Willie. She says she saw me on YouTube bashin' them Oakland cops. She says she was most impressed by the way I swung ol' Betsy. She says the Fleury Mérogis Prison guards also been clashin' with police. But the police just gassed 'em, herded 'em up, and sent 'em back to work. She says if I ever get out of jail, the guards got a place for me on their picket line.

THREE DAYS LATER, I meet my attorney in this crowded visitors' room. A silver-haired public defender who reminds me of Maurice Chevalier. The fucker tells me I ain't been arraigned yet 'cause the cops are still addin' up my charges. But I got at least twenty-five counts of aggravated battery and twenty-five counts of resisting arrest. And I got me a warrant from the UK with a buncha charges more. He says I could plead out for thirty years if I name all my contacts with Al Qaeda. That'll keep the world safe for democracy, he says.

When Maurice is done talkin', he punch dials his cell phone and says I got me an admirer. A fine-boned countess of Spanish descent that only a Frenchman can handle. 'Cause the madame seems pretty high maintenance and looks like she got refined standards. He says, "Ooh la la" as he hands me the phone.

The dude's got some kinda TV on his phone and I see me ol' Jessica on it. And it looks like she's holdin' a cell phone too 'cause her face is kinda wobbly. But it ain't hard to see she been pining away just like Mona Lisa. The bitch musta heard I'm an international star now. And she *still* don't wanna share me with no groupies.

Well, ol' Jessica may be pissed, but I got her in the palm of my hand. And when she says "Head-ward" in her throaty-ass voice, I rub the phone on my woody.

"Head-ward," she repeats. "What have you done?! What on earth have you done?!"

"I done topped the charts, Miss Jimenez," I say. "My ratings are *outta* this world."

"Head-ward, you are in *jail*. The biggest jail in Europe."

"Gonna cut you in on the action," I say. "Ol' Pomeroy done raised the bar."

Well, Jessica she keeps poutin' like maybe I'm talkin' smack. Like she's too high maintenance to be satisfied with phone sex. "Head-ward," she says, "I have had calls from the Department of Homeland Security. I have had calls from the CIA. They think you're a terrorist, mi amor, and not a deluded fool."

Ol' Jessica, she starts mutterin' in Spanish and Pomeroy starts to get irked. Just 'cause ol' Charlemagne done set me up don't mean we ain't still got a deal. So I tell her my groupies are so juiced up that they're gonna be stormin' the jail. If the bitch is gonna put Pomeroy down, I'm gonna keep her jealous.

Well, ol' Jessica she kinda pauses then her voice gets taut. "Dios mio," she says. "Such groupies you have. They're demonstrating in Zurich. They're demonstrating in Tel Aviv. They're demonstrating in Rio, Berlin, and Quebec. Topless women all shouting, 'Free Pomeroy.' I have never seen anything *like* it, Head-ward. They're calling you a hero of the people and a protector of femininity."

"Can you get me outta jail, Miss Jimenez? Femininity *needs* my ass."

"Head-ward, are you serious? Those are ignorant peasant girls. They're a long way from having a vision for womanhood."

"I'm serious 'bout gettin' my butt outta jail."

Ol' Jessica drops her gaze and her face looks kinda mellow. "Head-ward," she says, "that may not be for a long long time." I hear her voice catch and damn if the bitch ain't cryin'. "But I will try, mi amor. I promise you I will try."

Ol' Jessica, she starts rubbin' her eyes and my peewee TV goes blank. Guess I got her so stoked for a Pomeroy poke that the bitch done dropped her phone. And ran off to diddle her twat. So I give the phone back to ol' Maurice who wants to discuss my charges.

Maurice kisses his fingers and says, "Ooh la la." And he says he can make me a deal.

THE GUARDS MARCH ME through the courtyard as they're takin' me back to my range. And them cons are still hollerin' out the windows and throwin' their trash on the ground. And some of them jailbirds are cheerin' me 'cause they know I become a star. Guess they done seen my bare-titted groupies on their range televisions. So I throw back my head while I'm marchin' along and sing me a coupla more verses.

Well, I'm in a noisy dungeon
'Cause my cock's too hot to tame
But my groupies are all lungin'
And they're callin' out my name.
Yes, them bitches all got clit-ons
And their clits are hard as steel
So they're gonna rush this prison
Like they're stormin' the Bastille.

Well, I got me a captive audience now, but the New World Order don't listen as good. So I ain't sure ol' Jessica can help me none. And I ain't sure Oxsana can help me none. But that ain't gettin' ol' Pomeroy down—not by a long shot it ain't. 'Cause *Ants in My Pants* is playin' everywhere.

Song Credits

This Land is Your Land
Written by Woodie Guthrie, 1940
Popularized by Woody Guthrie

God Bless America
Written by Irving Berlin, 1918
Popularized by Kate Smith

Masters of War
Written by Bob Dylan, 1962-63
Performed by Bob Dylan

Battle Hymn of the Republic
Written by Julia Ward Howe, 1861
Popularized by Pomeroy and The Mormon
    Tabernacle Choir

A Hard Rain's a Gonna Fall
Written by Bob Dylan, 1962
Performed by Bob Dylan

Clean Cut Kid
Written by Bob Dylan, 1985
Performed by Bob Dylan
Whistled by Sam the Poontang Man

I-Feel-Like-I'm-Fixin'-to-Die Rag
Written by Country Joe McDonald, 1965
Performed by Country Joe and the Fish

Working Class Hero
Written by John Lennon, 1971
Performed by John Lennon
Yodeled by Sam the Poontang Man

Wake Up Little Susie
Written by Felice and Boudleaux Bryant, 1957
Popularized by The Everly Brothers
Politicized by The Black Bloc Anarchists

Sweet Molly Malone
Written by James Yorkston, 1883
Popularized by The Dubliners

Kiss Me Blarney Stones
Written by Mike Nugent and Ted Rypel, 2010, 2011, 2012
Popularized by Mike Nugent and Ted Rypel & The Pop Tarts

Ballad of the Green Berets
Written by Robin Moore and Staff Sergeant Barry Sadler,
    1966
First performed by Staff Sergeant Barry Sadler

Fortunate Son
Written by John Fogerty, 1969
Performed by Credence Clearwater Revival

Will Ye Go Lassie Go
Written by Frank McPeake, 1950
Popularized by The Clancey Brothers and Tommy Makem

Danny Boy
Written by Frederick Weatherly, 1910
Popularized by Elsie Griffin

The Green Fields of France
Written by Eric Bogle, 1976
Popularized by The Furey Brothers and Davey Arthur

The Happy Wanderer
Words by Florenz Friedrich Sigismund, 19th Century
Tune by Friedrich-Wilhelm Möller, 1945
Popularized by The Obernkirchen Children's Choir

Thank Heaven for Little Girls
Written by Alan Jay Lerner and Frederick Loewe, 1957
Popularized by Maurice Chevelier
Depopularized by Pomeroy
Frère Jacques
Children's nursery rhyme believed to have been first
    published in 1811.

License to Kill
Written by Bob Dylan, 1983
First performed by Bob Dylan
Popularized by Oxsana Chaplinsky

Ants in My Pants
Written by Edward Beasley, AKA Samson, Crokett,
    Pomeroy, 2002, 2003, 2004, 2005, 2006, 2007, 2008,
    2009, 2010, 2011, 2012, 2013, 2014
Popularized by Pomeroy and Sam the Poontang Man

Acknowledgements

First, I would like to thank E. Branden Hart, Robert Rossi, and Kari Totah for providing the inspiration for the Pomeroy character. To them, I have dedicated this book. I am also grateful to Mary Hanna, my wife, and Catherine Hanna, my mother, for supporting me in my ambition to publish this second book.

I am grateful to the following members of my critique group for their many comments on the Pomeroy stories: Lisa Meltzer Penn, Chris Wachlin, Bardi Rosman Koodrin, and Ann Foster. The stories are stronger because of them. And I'm particularly grateful to Elise Frances Miller and Darlene Frank for helping me promote the book.
I would like to thank Craig and Derrick, the proprietors of Reach & Teach in San Mateo, CA, where the Pomeroy stories were first read aloud. And kudos to Chris Wachlin, Jim Hartley, Audrey Kalman, and Maurine Killough for their colorful portrayals of Pomeroy and his gang.

Again, special thanks goes to Tory Hartmann, my publisher, friend, and chief editor. Without her, this book would not have been possible.